THE CASE OF
THE RELUCTANT MODEL

ERLE STANLEY GARDNER

THE CASE OF
THE RELUCTANT MODEL

UNABRIDGED

PAN BOOKS LTD · LONDON

First published
in Great Britain 1967 by William Heinemann Ltd.
This edition published 1970 by Pan Books Ltd,
33 Tothill Street, London, S.W.1

ISBN 0 330 02552 X

Printed in Great Britain by
Richard Clay (The Chaucer Press), Ltd, Bungay, Suffolk

FOREWORD

The Honourable James M. Carter, one of the judges of the United States District Court in San Diego, is one of the most competent trial judges I know and an outstanding humanitarian to boot.

Not only do police and penologists respect Judge Carter but the men he sentences to prison, for the most part, share that respect.

For one thing, Judge Carter's thinking isn't only in multiples of five, ten, or fifteen years as is the case with so many judges who pass out sentences. He thinks of each long year as a twelve-month period. For another thing, after Judge Carter sentences an individual, he has that man brought back into his chambers. There the judge divests himself of his judicial robes and talks man to man. He explains to the individual why he is being sent to prison and why he fixed the term he did. He tells the man he wants him to make good while in prison, that if he has any trouble the judge wants to know about it. Judge Carter asks the defendant to keep in touch with him.

Word percolates around, therefore, that Judge Carter is not only a just judge, but is a great humanitarian.

It was that reputation which caused an American Indian, the mother of a young man who had been convicted by Army court-martial of murder without malice and who was serving a twenty-year term, to write Judge Carter that she felt an injustice had been done.

Knowing of my interest in such matters, Judge Carter suggested that she write me and then kept in touch with me to find out what I learned about the case.

At my request, the mother sent me a transcript of the evidence and, as I studied it, it became apparent that the question of whether there ever had been any murder in the case depended upon an interesting medical conclusion. The consulting pathologist who testified at the military trial had not seen the deceased but based his testimony on the findings of the autopsy surgeon and had, apparently, gone farther than the autopsy surgeon was willing to go.

For some years I have been greatly impressed with the importance of legal medicine, its place in the administration of justice and the necessity for a better understanding on the part of the public of what it is and how it functions.

From time to time I have dedicated books to outstanding figures in the field of legal medicine.

So I chose, at random, several of these persons to whom I had dedicated books. I had my secretaries copy all the medical evidence in the transcript and send it to these people asking for their opinion on the medico-legal aspects of the case. (Since the consulting pathologist called by the prosecution had based his opinion solely on the records of the autopsy, these experts whom I called into the case had *exactly* the same factual evidence from the protocol and the transcript that this consulting pathologist had used in reaching his opinion.)

I limited my selection to the number of experts who could be given legible carbon copies from one run on an electric typewriter because the material was so voluminous it presented a major secretarial undertaking.

These experts, top men in their field, many of them working day and night, responded with opinions. As fast as these opinions were received I had them copied and sent out in a round-robin to all of the persons connected with the case.

Some of these experts were so conscientious that they refrained from reading the opinions of the other experts until after they had formulated their own opinion, lest they be influenced by the others' thinking.

It was an exacting job, reviewing the mass of medical evidence and reaching an opinion; particularly in view of the fact that these experts knew their opinion would be publicized to the extent of asking for a review of the case.

I am proud of the manner in which these busy men went to work studying the evidence in this case of a penniless American Indian who had been convicted of a murder, which, it soon developed, had in all probability never been committed.

Almost at once these experts pointed out a peculiar discrepancy. The consulting pathologist had acted upon a mistaken assumption that certain significant hemorrhagic conditions had existed, whereas the autopsy surgeon had not only failed to find such hemorrhagic conditions, but had considered their absence a significant point in reaching his conclusions.

For a period of months reports came in; well-reasoned, carefully thought-out reports. And the majority were to the effect that under the peculiar circumstances of the case it was quite possible the victim had died a natural death.

The victim was an elderly, quarrelsome man who had the reputation of being the village drunkard and engaging in altercations when he was inebriated. The post-mortem findings showed beyond question that he was pretty well intoxicated at the time of his death and his reputation indicated that not only was he abusive and quarrelsome under those circumstances, but that he had probably picked a fight with the young Indian and could well have met his death not as a result of that fight, but some time later and from natural causes.

The Indian had been on a drinking spree with a companion and upon subsequently regaining his senses had insufficient recollection of what had happened to be of any help.

Listed in alphabetical order, the forensic experts, many of whom are lawyers as well as doctors, who submitted detailed reports were:

Lester Adelson, MD
Pathologist and Chief Deputy Coroner
County of Cuyahoga Coroner's Office
Cleveland, Ohio

Francis Camps, MD
London, England

Daniel J. Condon, MD
Medical Examiner of Maricopa County
Phoenix, Arizona

Russell S. Fisher, MD
Chief Medical Examiner of
Baltimore, Maryland

Richard Ford, MD
Professor of Legal Medicine
Harvard University
Boston, Massachusetts

S. R. Gerber, MD
Coroner, County of Cuyahoga
Cleveland, Ohio

Milton Helpern, MD
City of New York,
Office of Chief Medical Examiner
New York, New York

Joseph A. Jachimczyk, MD
Office of Medical Examiner of
Harris County
Court House
Houston, Texas

Alvin V. Majoska, MD, Pathologist
Honolulu, Hawaii

LeMoyne Snyder, MD
San Francisco, California

Under the new revised miltary code many authorities feel that the military system of criminal justice approaches the ideal method of handling criminal cases. The rights of the accused are protected, but procedural technicalities are designed to facilitate proof and ensure complete fairness, not as technical loopholes.

Even after conviction and the expiration of the time for appeal, a reviewing board makes an annual check-up on the prisoner and the rules are sufficiently flexible so that many matters concerning the prisoner can be given consideration at the discretion of the board.

In this case, the reports of the medical experts were passed on to the reviewing board and the careful attention given by the board, the courtroom interest shown in every phase of the case, has been most reassuring.

Judge Carter made several trips from his residence in San Diego to my ranch at Temecula, interrupted his busy schedule to make a careful analysis of the evidence and made a special trip to the institution where the young man was confined, to interview him.

The file in this case has grown to huge proportions. The man-hours spent in the investigation and presentation are staggering.

Even a wealthy man could hardly afford to consult such an array of medical talent. Yet these men furnished their services gratuitously to review the case of a penniless Indian boy. Devoted to the cause of justice, these men took no count of the cost.

In these days we hear much of conflicting ideologies. Perhaps, just as we take the air we breathe for granted, many of us fail to realize the advantages we enjoy under the concept of justice which is so much a part of our traditional background.

And so I salute the military code in which ultimate justice takes precedence over technicalities, and I dedicate this book to those men who gave so unselfishly of their time to investigate the case of a penniless Indian.

ERLE STANLEY GARDNER

CHAPTER ONE

Perry Mason opening the door of his private office, grinned at Della Street, his confidential secretary, and said, 'All right, so I'm late.'

Della Street, glancing at her wristwatch, smiled indulgently. 'Okay, so you're late! And if you want to sleep late I don't know anyone who's more entitled to do so – only I'm afraid we're going to have to buy a new carpet for the reception room.'

Mason's eyes were puzzled. 'A new carpet?'

'This one's getting worn out.'

'What do you mean, Della?'

'You have a client who has been waiting since one minute before nine o'clock when Gertie opened up the office. The trouble is he won't sit still. He's pacing the office at the rate of five miles an hour, looking at his watch every fifteen or twenty seconds and demanding to know where you are.'

'Who is it?' Mason asked.

'Lattimer Rankin.'

Mason frowned. 'Rankin,' he said, 'Rankin. . . . Isn't he the one who has something to do with pictures?'

'The big art dealer,' Della Street said.

'Oh, yes, I place him now,' Mason told her. 'He's the one who testified as to the value of the painting in the civil suit – and gave us a picture. What the devil did we do with that picture, Della?'

'It's gathering dust in the storeroom off the law library. That is, it was until five minutes past nine this morning.'

'And then what?' Mason asked.

'Then,' Della Street said, 'I got it and hung it just to the right of the door where a client will see it when he sits in the client's chair.'

Della Street indicated the painting.

11

'Good girl,' Mason said approvingly. 'I wonder if you've hung it upside-down.'

'It's all upside-down if you ask me,' she said, 'but at least we've got it there, and there's a label on the back of the picture that has the name of Lattimer Rankin and the address of his place of business. If the label's right side up, the picture is right side up.

'So if he looks at you disapprovingly and says, "Mr Mason, you've got the picture upside-down," you can look right back at him and say, "Mr Rankin, you've got your label upside-down."'

'Fair enough,' Mason said. 'Let's get him off the tenter-hooks. Bring him in, Della. I knew I didn't have any early morning appointments so I was cheating a little bit on office hours.'

'I told him you were on your way,' Della Street said, 'that you'd been detained in a traffic jam.'

'How did you know?' Mason asked, grinning.

'Telepathy,' she said.

'Do you plan to read my mind all the time?' he asked.

'I'd be afraid to *all* the time,' she said archly. 'I'll get Mr Rankin in before the carpet is entirely threadbare.'

A few moments later Della Street opened the door and Lattimer Rankin, a tall, dark, grim-faced individual, with piercing grey eyes, came striding into the room as though he had been walking in a marathon contest and didn't want to break his stride. He moved across to Mason's desk, gripped the lawyer's hand with his own huge, bony hand, swept the office in a brief survey, said, 'I see you've hung my picture. A lot of people didn't appreciate that artist's work but I'm glad to tell you it's going across very nicely now. I knew it would. He has power, harmony. Mason, I want to sue a man for libel and slander.'

'No, you don't,' Mason said.

Mason's comment caused Rankin to straighten up. 'I think you failed to understand me,' he said with cold emphasis. 'I have been slandered. I wish to retain you to file suit immediately. I want to sue Collin M. Durant for half a million dollars.'

'Sit down,' Mason said.

Rankin settled himself in the client's chair with the stiffness of a carpenter's rule being folded up. The man seemed absolutely rigid except at the joints.

'I want the suit to get all the publicity we can give it,' he said. 'I want to drive Collin M. Durant out of town. The man is incompetent, he's a fourflusher, a publicity-seeker, an unethical competitor, and he has none of the instincts of a gentleman.'

'You want to sue him for half a million dollars,' Mason said.

'Yes, sir.'

'And you want lots of publicity.'

'Yes, sir.'

'You want to claim that he damaged your professional reputation.'

'That's right.'

'To the tune of half a million dollars.'

'Yes, sir.'

'You will,' Mason pointed out, 'have to specify the manner in which he did this.'

'He did it by intimating that I am incompetent, that my judgement is unsound, that I have victimized one of my customers.'

'And to whom did he make these statements? How many people?' Mason asked.

'I have long suspected that he has made them by innuendo to anyone who would listen, but now I have a very definite witness – a young woman named Maxine Lindsay.'

'And what did he say to Maxine Lindsay?'

'He said that a painting I had sold Otto Olney was a rank imitation and that any art dealer worthy of the name would have recognized it as such as soon as he saw it.'

'He made that statement only to Maxine Lindsay?'

'Yes.'

'In the presence of witnesses?'

'There were no other witnesses except Maxine. Under the circumstances you would hardly have expected any.'

'What circumstances?' Mason asked.

'He was engaged in trying to promote his own stock with the

13

young lady – making a pass, I believe is the popular expression.'

'Has she repeated the statement?' Mason asked. 'That is, has she spread it around any?'

'She has not. Maxine Lindsay is an art student. I was able to help her two or three times. I have given her some bargains on painting materials and she is grateful. She came to me at once and told me she thought I should know what Durant was doing. I knew, all right, but this was the first time I had had an opportunity to prove it.'

'All right,' Mason said, 'I will now repeat my statement. You don't want to sue.'

'I'm afraid I don't understand you,' Rankin said with formality. 'My credit certainly is good. My cheque book is here. I am prepared to give you a retainer. I want suit filed at once. I want to file suit for half a million dollars. Surely the courts are open to me, and if you don't wish to take my case—'

'Come on down to earth,' Mason said. 'Let's talk facts.'

'Very well, go ahead and talk facts.'

Mason said, 'So far, Maxine Lindsay knows that Collin Durant said you sold Otto Olney a picture which wasn't genuine ... By the way, how much did you get for the picture?'

'Thirty-five hundred dollars.'

'All right,' Mason said, 'Maxine Lindsay knows what Durant said. You file suit for half a million dollars. The newspapers publish the story of the suit. Tomorrow morning a million readers will know that an art dealer named Lattimer Rankin has been accused of peddling a phoney picture. That's *all* they'll remember.'

'Nonsense!' Rankin stormed. 'They will know that I am suing Collin Durant, that at last someone has had the courage to bring that bounder to account.'

'No, they won't,' Mason said. 'They will read about the suit but they won't remember very much about it except that an art expert said you had been peddling worthless art for thirty-five hundred dollars to a valued customer.'

Rankin frowned, blinked his eyes rapidly several times, then brought them to hard focus on Mason's face.

'You mean to say I must sit here and let that unspeakable

14

cad go around making statements that no reputable dealer would make? Hang it, Mason! The man isn't an expert, he's a dealer, and if you ask me, he's a damned poor dealer at that!'

'I'm not asking you,' Mason said, 'and you're not making that statement, because the first thing you know Durant might turn around and sue *you* for defamation of character. Now, you came up here for advice. I'm going to give you that advice. It probably isn't the advice you want, but it's the advice you need.

'When you sue a man for defamation of character, in a business way you put your own reputation right out on the line. You have to submit to a deposition and the lawyer on the other side starts asking you questions. Suppose I start asking you those questions first: *Did* you sell Otto Olney a phoney painting?'

'Absolutely not.'

'How do you know?'

'Because I know the painting. I know the artist. I know his work. I know his style. I know art, Mason. Hang it, I couldn't stay in business ten minutes if I didn't. That picture is absolutely genuine.'

'All right,' Mason said. 'So, instead of having you sue Durant for half a million dollars' damages, claiming that he has damaged your reputation, and putting you in the position of going on the witness stand and trying to prove that Durant's statement was made with malice and that it undermined the confidence of your customers, actual and potential, we go to see Otto Olney.'

'What good does that do?' Rankin asked.

'We get Otto Olney, as the owner of the painting, to sue Durant claiming that Durant has disparaged the value of his picture by making a statement that it was spurious. Olney alleges that he paid thirty-five hundred dollars for the picture, that it was well worth twice that amount or seven thousand dollars, and that the aspersions cast upon the painting by Collin Durant have damaged him in the amount of seven thousand dollars.

'Then,' Mason went on, 'people reading the newspaper know that a man with the standing of Otto Olney has accused

15

Durant of being a malicious spite-peddler, that he is incompetent as an art appraiser or he is a liar.

'We get the newspapermen interested, we get a photograph of the picture in question, and we have Olney call in some expert art appraiser who pronounces the picture genuine. Then we have a picture taken of you, the art appraiser, and Otto Olney, all standing beside the picture shaking hands, beaming at each other. The general public reading the article will come to the conclusion that Collin M. Durant is a very shady character indeed; that you are a reputable art dealer, that the experts back up your judgement, and that your customers are completely satisfied.

'The only thing that is in issue is the authenticity of the painting, not your reputation, not the amount of *your* damages, not anything that can be dredged up from your background that you might not want to have publicized.'

Rankin blinked his eyes rapidly, thrust his hand into his breast pocket, pulled out a cheque book, said, 'It's a pleasure to work with a real expert, Mr Mason. Will a thousand dollars be an adequate retainer?'

'A thousand dollars will be about five hundred dollars too much,' Mason said, 'depending, of course, on what you want to have done and how serious this matter is.'

'The matter is very serious indeed,' Rankin said. 'Collin M. Durant is a wise guy, one of these smart-alecks, a know-it-all, a talker. He isn't content to make acquaintances in the art world and build up his reputation slowly and by merit. He is, instead, bent upon trying to build his own reputation by tearing down the reputation of others. I am not the only one who has been the target of his innuendos and sneering comments, but I am perhaps the only one who has a very definite case in that a certain specific object of art which I sold has been definitely and positively branded as spurious by Durant to a witness who will testify.'

'How do you get along with Olney?' Mason asked. 'You sold him this one painting. Have you sold him any more?'

'Only the one. But I have every reason to believe he is very friendly.'

'Why only the one?' Mason asked. 'After you make a sale, don't you try to keep a man as a customer?'

'The point is that Olney is a rather peculiar individual with very definite tastes. At that particular time he wanted one painting and only one painting. Actually he commissioned me to buy that painting if I could find it, and I think he may have commissioned others as well.'

'What's the painting?' Mason asked.

'It's a Phellipe Feteet.'

'I'm afraid you'll have to enlighten me more than that,' Mason said.

'Phellipe Feteet is, or rather was, a Frenchman who went to the Philippines and started painting. His early work was rather mediocre. Then he developed what was to be his forte – pictures of natives in the shade with sunlit backgrounds.

'You may not have noticed it, Mr Mason, but there are very, very few painters who can get the true effect of sunlight. There are many reasons for this, one of which is that the canvas cannot transmit light; it only uses colours to suggest light. The contrast, therefore, between sunlight and shadow is seldom really emphasized in a painting. But in the work of Phellipe Feteet – that is, in his later years – he turned out pictures that were so vivid they have a terrific impact. The illusion of sunlight is so bright it is dazzling. You want to reach for a pair of dark glasses.

'Even studying his pictures, no one knows exactly how he did it. The man has a gift for this type of work. I don't think there are more than two dozen of his later pictures in existence, and so far only a few people really appreciate the man's work. But there is a growing sense of appreciation.

'You mention that Olney's picture was sold for thirty-five hundred dollars and is worth seven thousand. You had better up that latter figure materially. I sold him the picture for thirty-five hundred dollars. I would like to buy it back for ten thousand. I think I could sell it for fifteen. Five years from now it will be worth fifty.'

Mason grinned. 'All right,' he said, 'there's your answer. You go and see Otto Olney. You fix things up with him. You get a disinterested art expert to go out there and appraise the painting. You get Olney to sue Durant for disparaging his picture. You have the art expert offer Olney ten thousand dollars for the picture. That makes a story the newspapers can eat up. Olney files the suit. The suit is against Durant. You only come into it as the dealer who sold the picture and whose judgement is vindicated by an independent art expert. The fact that you sold a picture for thirty-five hundred dollars and the trade is now willing to pay ten thousand for it, the fact that the art expert appraises it as being worth three times what you charged for it a few years ago, makes everybody happy.

'The newspapers will want to know who Phellipe Feteet was and you can tell them the story of his pictures and the fact that they are going up in value every day. This will enhance the value of Olney's painting, will have a tendency to start a new vogue for the Feteet paintings, and Durant will be the one who is behind the eight ball.

'If the newspapers want to interview Durant, all he can do is reiterate his statement that the painting is spurious. At that time his story will give Olney more grounds for a law-suit, Durant's opinion will be at variance with the established art appraisers in the country, Olney will have a good cause of action, your damaged reputation won't enter into the litigation. In fact your reputation will actually be enhanced by all the newspaper publicity.

'How long before you can fix things up with Olney?'

'I shall call on Olney right away,' Rankin said, 'and I'll get George Lathan Howell, the noted art expert, to appraise the painting and—'

'Whoa, back up,' Mason interrupted. 'You don't get anybody to appraise anything until we are ready to release the newspaper publicity. That is why I asked you if you were sure the painting was genuine. If there is any room for doubt, we're going to have to handle things in another way. In a deal of this sort we have to fit our strategy to the facts.'

'You may rest assured the painting is a genuine Feteet,' Rankin said.

'Now there's one other point,' Mason said. 'We will have to prove that Durant said the painting was spurious.'

'But I told you about that. Maxine came to me. I have it direct from her own lips.'

'Send her to me,' Mason said. 'I want to tie her up with an affidavit. You can imagine what a fix we'd be in if we started

18

all this newspaper publicity and then fell down on our proof. Durant would then have you in a trap.

'To date, our only witness is Maxine Lindsay. We have to be certain we can depend on her.'

'We can depend on her with our lives,' Rankin said.

'You can get her to come in to the office here and give us an affidavit?' Mason asked.

'I'm certain of it.'

'How soon?'

'Any time you say.'

'Within an hour?'

'Well . . . right after lunch. How will that do?'

'That's okay,' Mason told him. 'You get in touch with Otto Olney. See how he feels about the situation, suggest that he file suit, and—'

'And retain you?' Rankin asked.

'Heavens, no,' Mason said. 'He's got his own lawyers. Let him instruct them to file the suit. I'll arrange the behind-the-scenes strategy, and that's all. You pay me for my advice, Olney pays his lawyers for filing the suit, and Durant pays in damages for trying to undermine the value of a painting – and the resultant publicity will build up your reputation all the more.'

Rankin said, 'Mr Mason, I am going to insist on making that cheque in an amount of a thousand dollars, and thank heaven I had the good sense to come to you rather than some attorney who would have let me tell him what *I* wanted *him* to do.'

Rankin filled out the cheque, handed it to Della Street, shook hands with Mason, and strode from the office.

Mason grinned at Della Street. 'Now then, take that damned picture down and put it back in the storeroom,' he said.

CHAPTER TWO

It was one-thirty in the afternoon when Della said, 'Your witness is out in the other office, Chief.'

'Witness?' Mason asked.

'The one on the spurious painting.'

'Oh,' Mason said, 'the young woman whom Durant was trying to impress by telling her Olney's painting was a phoney. I want to see if she'll stand up in court, so let's have a look at her, Della.'

'I've already looked at her.'

'How does she stack up?'

Della's eyes twinkled. 'She stacks.'

'How old?'

'Twenty-eight, twenty-nine, thirty.'

'Blonde, brunette, redhead?'

'Blonde.'

'Let's have a look,' Mason said.

'Coming right up,' Della Street told him, and left for the outer office to return in a moment with a very blue-eyed blonde who smiled somewhat diffidently.

'Maxine Lindsay,' Della Street said, 'and this is Mr Mason, Miss Lindsay.'

'How do you do?' she said, coming forward and giving him her hand with a quick, impulsive gesture. 'I've heard *so* much about you, Mr Mason! When Mr Rankin told me I was to see you I could hardly believe it.'

'I'm very pleased to meet you,' Mason said. 'Now, do you know why you're here, Miss Lindsay?'

'On account of Mr Durant?'

'That's right,' Mason said. 'Would you care to tell me about it?'

'You mean about the forged Feteet?'

'Was it forged?'

'All right,' Mason said, 'would you mind sitting down in that chair, Miss Lindsay, and recounting the conversation?'

She dropped into the chair, smiled at Della Street,

smoothed her dress, said, 'Where shall I begin?'

'When was it?'

'A week ago.'

'Where?'

'On Mr Olney's yacht.'

'You're a friend of his?'

'In a way.'

'And Durant?'

'He was there.'

'A friend of Olney's?'

'Well,' she said, 'perhaps I'd better explain. It was sort of an artists' party.'

'Olney is an artist?'

'No, he likes artists. He likes art. He likes to talk art. He likes to discuss pictures.'

'And he buys them?'

'Sometimes.'

'But he doesn't paint?'

'No, he'd like to but he can't. He has good ideas but poor talent.'

'And you're an artist?'

'I'd like to be. I've had a little success with some of my pictures.'

'And that's how you knew Mr Olney?'

Her eyes met Mason's frankly. 'No,' she said, 'I don't think that's the reason he invited me.'

'Why did he invite you?' Mason asked. 'A personal interest?'

'Not in that way,' she said. 'I've done some modelling. He met me when I was posing for one of the artists. I did pretty good at modelling until I became a little ... well, a little busty. So then I decided I'd go in for art.'

'Does being busty disqualify you as a model?' Mason asked. 'In the depths of my ignorance I thought it was the other way around.'

She smiled. 'Photographers like big busts; artists, as a rule, like a delicacy of figure. I began to lose out on the high-class artist modelling and I wasn't going to pose for the cheaper photographic work. The high-class photographer is even more choosy than the artist.'

21

'So you took up painting?' Mason asked.

'Of a sort, yes.'

'You're making a living at it?'

'Of a sort, yes.'

'You hadn't done any painting before?' Mason asked. 'Any art school or——?'

'It's not that kind of painting,' she said. 'I do portraits.'

'I thought that took quite a bit of training,' Mason said.

'Not the way I do it. I take a photograph, a low-key photograph, blow it up to twenty-two by twenty-eight, and just barely print it. I have it so the image is only plain enough to serve as a guide. Then I go over this image with transparent paint. Then, with that as a base, I use oils to make a finished portrait. I've been rather successful.'

'But Olney was more interested in your——'

She smiled. 'I think he was interested in my attitude towards art and . . . well, towards posing.'

'And what's the attitude?' Mason asked.

'If you're going to pose,' she said, 'why not be frank about it? I never did have any personal hypocrisy and . . . well, anyway, one time when I was modelling I got to talking with Mr Olney about his philosophy of life and my philosophy of life. . . . He'd dropped in to see the artist – and the next thing I knew I was invited to one of his parties.'

'That was when the painting was discussed?'

'Oh, no, that was later, a week ago.'

'All right, now tell us about that party. You were talking with Durant?'

'Yes.'

'He was telling you about Olney's paintings?'

'Not about Olney's paintings. He was discussing art dealers.'

'And did he discuss Lattimer Rankin?'

'That was the one he was primarily discussing.'

'Can you tell me how the conversation came about?'

She said, 'I think Durant was trying to impress me, but he was . . . well, we were out on the deck and . . . he was becoming quite personal . . . I have been very grateful to Mr Rankin. I think Durant sensed that and resented it.'

'Go ahead.'

'He discussed Mr Rankin, made some remark about him

that I thought was just a little, well, a little – it would have been what you would call catty if he had been a woman.'

'But he wasn't a woman,' Mason said.

'Definitely not!' she observed with emphasis.

'I take it his hands were restless?' Mason asked.

'All masculine hands are restless,' she said casually. 'His were persistent.'

'And then?'

'I told him that I liked Mr Rankin, that Rankin had befriended me and I liked him, and he said, "All right, like him if you want to as a friend but don't buy any art from him or you'll get stuck." '

'And what did you say to that?'

'I asked him what he meant by it.'

'And what did he say?'

'He said that Rankin either had lousy judgement or victimized his customers, that one of the paintings on the yacht which had been sold by Rankin to Olney was a fake.'

'You asked him which one?'

'Yes.'

'And he told you?'

'Yes, the Phellipe Feteet that was hanging in the main saloon.'

'That's quite a yacht?' Mason asked.

'It's quite a yacht,' she said. 'It was designed to go anyplace the owner wanted to go, around the world – anywhere.'

'Olney goes around the world?'

'I don't think so. He does a little cruising once in a while but primarily he uses it for parties where ... where he can entertain his artistic friends. He lives on board a great deal of the time.'

'He doesn't have his artist friends at his home?' Mason asked.

'I don't think so.'

'Why?'

'I don't think his wife approves.'

'You've met her?'

'Definitely not.'

'But you do know Olney?'

'Yes.'

'All right,' Mason said. 'I have to be crude about this. You're going to be a witness.'

'I don't want to be a witness.'

'You just about *have* to be a witness,' Mason said. 'A statement was made to you. You're going to have to repeat that statement. Now then, what I want to know is whether cross-examination could bring out anything that would be personally embarrassing.'

'That depends on the cross-examination,' she said, again meeting his eyes frankly. 'I'm twenty-nine years old. I don't think any girl twenty-nine years old could be cross-examined without—'

'Wait a minute,' Mason said,' don't get me wrong. I'll get right down to specific statements. Is there any romantic attachment between you and Lattimer Rankin?'

Her laugh was spontaneous. 'Heavens, no! Lattimer Rankin thinks art, dreams art, and eats art. His interest in me is as an artist. He has secured me commissions on a few portraits. He's a real friend. But the idea of any romance in Lattimer Rankin's mind— No, Mr Mason. Definitely no.'

'All right,' Mason said, 'there's one more question. How about Otto Olney?'

Her eyes narrowed slightly. 'I can't be sure about Olney.'

'You know whether you've had any romantic interludes with him.'

'There haven't been any romantic interludes,' she said, 'but he notices figures – and I have a figure.'

'Have you ever been out with him alone?'

'No.'

'No romantic discussions?'

'None. Except that ... well, if I were out alone with him he'd make passes.'

'How do you know?'

'Just on the basis of experience.'

'But you've never been out alone with him?'

'No.'

'And he hasn't made any passes?'

'No.'

'Now, let's not misunderstand each other,' Mason said.

24

'That's one place where you and I can't possibly afford to have any misunderstanding.

'I don't know this man, Durant, but if he starts fighting he'll get detectives. He'll prowl into your past as well as your present.'

'I take it,' she said, meeting his eyes, 'that no matter what he finds out he can't use any of it unless it pertains to Rankin or Olney.'

'Or to the art expert, George Lathan Howell,' Mason said, consulting his notes.

She said, 'Mr Howell is very, very nice.'

'All right,' Mason said, 'let's come right down to it. He's very nice. You know him, he knows you?'

'Yes.'

'Any romance?'

'I could lie,' she said.

'Here, or on the witness-stand?'

'Both.'

'I wouldn't,' Mason said.

She hesitated a moment, then again the blue eyes, frank and steady, met Mason's. 'Yes,' she said.

'Yes, what?'

'Yes, romance.'

'All right,' Mason told her. 'I'm going to try to protect you as much as possible. I've got to put through a phone call right away.'

Mason nodded to Della Street. 'Get Lattimer Rankin on the phone.'

A moment later when Della Street nodded, Mason picked up the telephone on his desk, said, 'Mason talking, Rankin. You were speaking about George Lathan Howell as an art expert. I have an idea it might be better to get some other art expert.'

'What's the matter?' Rankin asked. 'Isn't Howell okay? He's the best man I know of, and I—'

'It has nothing to do with his professional qualifications,' Mason interrupted, 'and I'm not able to give you a reason. I simply have to advise you as your attorney. What other expert do you know who would be a good man?'

'There's Corliss Kenner,' Rankin said after a moment.

'Who's he?'

'*She*. A darned good art expert. A little young, but she certainly knows her onions and I'd take her word on a picture just as readily as I would that of anyone in the business.'

'That's fine,' Mason told him. 'Does she have the hatchet-faced type of competency or—'

'Heavens, no!' Rankin interrupted. 'She's terribly attractive. She's a smart dresser, well-groomed, swell figure—'

'How old?'

'Lord, I don't know. In the thirties somewhere.'

'Middle, latter part?'

'No, I'd say about the first part.'

'How about using her?' Mason asked.

'I think that would be fine. Of course, I've been thinking, Mason, that would be up to Olney. He'd probably want to call in his own appraiser but – I have an idea he'd rather have her than anyone.'

'All right, that's fine,' Mason said. 'Just a moment.'

Mason held his hand over the phone, looked at Maxine Lindsay with a smile. 'I take it,' he said, 'there's no reason why cross-examination in a case where Corliss Kenner was an art expert would prove embarrassing in any way.'

Her eyes were smiling. 'There is no reason why it would prove embarrassing in *any* way,' she said.

'Okay,' Mason said into the telephone, 'forget Howell and suggest Corliss Kenner. I'm getting an affidavit from Maxine Lindsay. She isn't particularly anxious to get mixed into it but she'll ride along.'

'She's a good kid,' Rankin said, 'and while of course her technique is somewhat mechanical, I'm going to be able to do a lot for her. Tell her I'm getting her another commission for two children.'

'I'll tell her,' Mason said, and hung up.

'May I ask why the affidavit?' Maxine Lindsay asked.

'The affidavit,' Mason said, looking her straight in the eyes, 'is to be sure that you don't lead us down a garden pathway.

'You tell me certain things. I advise a client on the basis of those things. I have to assume that if and when you get into court and get on the witness-stand you will testify to those

26

same things that you have told me. If you don't, my client would be in serious difficulties.'

She nodded.

'Therefore,' Mason said, 'I like to have an affidavit from a person who is going to be a key witness. That affidavit is a statement under oath. If you should subsequently repudiate your story, you would then be guilty of perjury, just the same as if you had sworn falsely on the witness-stand.'

Her face showed relief. 'Oh,' she said, 'if *that's* all, I'll be glad to give you the affidavit.'

Mason nodded to Della Street, said, 'Write out the affidavit, Della. Get her to sign it and be sure she raises her right hand and swears.'

Maxine Lindsay said, 'I won't let you down, Mr Mason, if that's all that's worrying you. I don't like to get mixed into it but if I have to, I have to ... I won't let you down. I've never let anyone down. I don't do things that way.'

'I'm satisfied you don't,' Mason said, taking the out-stretched hand. 'Now you go with Miss Street and she'll get the affidavit and have you sign it.'

She hesitated a moment. 'If anything should come up in connection with this, can I reach you on the phone?'

'By calling Miss Street,' Mason said. 'Do you anticipate something will come up?'

'It might.'

'Then just call this office and ask for Della Street.'

'And if it should be an emergency, and after office hours or on a weekend?'

Mason regarded her thoughtfully. 'You can call the Drake Detective Agency. Their offices are on this floor. They are open twenty-four hours a day, seven days a week. They can usually reach me.'

'Thank you,' she said, and turned to Della Street.

Mason watched them as they left the office. His forehead was creased in a frown.

Abruptly he picked up his phone, said to the switchboard operator, 'Get me Paul Drake, Gertie, please.'

A moment later when Mason had the private detective on the line he said, 'A former artist's model by the name of Maxine Lindsay, Paul. She's now doing some portrait work of

her own. She became a little too busty for the sort of modelling she likes to do. Lattimer Rankin, the art dealer, has been
sponsoring her, but I don't want him to have any idea of an
investigation is being made. I want her general background,
Paul.'

'How old?' Drake asked.

'Late twenties, blonde, blue-eyed, well built, frank, poised.'

'I'll get right on it,' Drake promised.

'I was quite certain you would,' Mason said dryly. 'If she
should try to reach me through you after hours, find out what
she wants and if it sounds important relay the information.'

'Okay, will do. That's all?'

'That,' Mason said, 'is all,' and hung up.

CHAPTER THREE

Shortly after four o'clock Della Street said, 'Mr Olney's
lawyer is on the line, Chief. He wants to talk with you.'

Mason nodded, picked up the telephone, said. 'Perry Mason
speaking.'

'This is Roy Hollister, Mason, of Warton, Warton, Cosgrove and Hollister. We're attorneys for Otto Olney.

'It seems that a client of yours has advised Mr Olney that
an art dealer by the name of Durant has made a public statement to the effect that Mr Olney's favourite painting is a
forgery. Do you know anything about it?'

'I know a great deal about it,' Mason said. 'I have an affidavit from a witness who is willing to go on the stand and
swear that Durant told her a painting purportedly by Phellipe
Feteet, and which I believe was sold Otto Olney by Lattimer
Rankin, who is a client of mine, is a fake.'

'Doesn't that give Rankin a cause of action against Durant?'
Hollister asked.

'I would think so,' Mason said. 'I would certainly think he
could sue Durant for slander.'

'Well?' Hollister asked.

Mason said. 'Such an action would be for damage to his professional reputation and would put in issue not only whether the painting is genuine but Rankin's professional reputation. It also would necessitate showing that Durant was actuated by malice in making his statement and that it was not an honest mistake of opinion.

'If you ever tried a slander case you'll know some of the legal pitfalls – and the public would always remember Lattimer Rankin as the art dealer whose integrity was questioned by another art dealer . . . I don't intend to have my client walk into that trap.'

'What do you intend to do?'

'Nothing,' Mason said.

'Apparently Rankin thinks that Otto Olney should sue Durant.'

'Doubtless he does.'

'Well, we feel Rankin should wash his own dirty linen,' Hollister snapped. 'We don't want our client to be a cat's-paw for Rankin or for anyone else.'

'Neither do I,' Mason told him, his voice almost casual. 'However, if Olney wants to shut Durant up, all he has to do is to file suit to prove that the picture is genuine. The picture itself is all that would be in issue in *that* suit.'

'I don't know that he cares to go to those lengths to protect Rankin's reputation,' Hollister said.

'I certainly wouldn't think that he should,' Mason said. 'If he were my client I would advise him not to.'

'Well then, what's all the shooting about?' Hollister asked.

'But if he *were* my client,' Mason went on, 'I would advise him that unless somebody stopped Durant from making those statements he was going to have his painting branded as a fraud, he was going to have himself labelled, at least in the popular mind, as a prime sucker. I don't know enough about your client's business position to know whether such a reputation would damage him or not. I have an idea it would.'

There was a moment of silence.

'Well?' Mason asked.

'I'm thinking it over,' Hollister said.

'Take all the time you want,' Mason told him.

'You're not planning to have Lattimer Rankin file suit?'

'As long as he's my client he isn't going to file suit. He could put himself right out on the end of the limb very easily. Do you want me to send you a copy of an affidavit executed by Maxine Lindsay?'

'Who's she?'

'The person to whom Durant made the statement about the painting.'

'I'd like very much to have a copy of that affidavit,' Hollister said, 'and then I think I'd like to sleep on it. I'll call you first thing in the morning.'

'Okay,' Mason said, 'we'll send the affidavit right over.'

He looked up from the phone to make sure Della Street was listening on her extension and taking notes.

'My secretary will take care of it immediately,' Mason said, and hung up.

Della Street smiled. 'Well, *he* certainly executed an about-face,' she said. 'He called you up to tell you you couldn't use him or his client as cat's-paws.'

Mason grinned.

'Tell me, Chief,' she asked, 'could you get hurt in a suit of this kind?'

'My client could,' Mason said.

'So your strategy begins to unfold.' Della Street smiled. 'How about Olney? Could he get hurt?'

Mason laughed. 'A wealthy contractor who has a lawyer retained by the month – how could he?'

'And Durant gets called to account in a case where he hasn't a legal leg to stand on except the painting itself, and it doesn't cost Rankin anything except the retainer he paid. That seems to me to be a pretty good deal – for Rankin.'

'Well,' Mason said, grinning, 'that's what he wanted to pay me for, wasn't it? And remember, Olney has his own very competent lawyers.'

CHAPTER FOUR

Ten-thirty Tuesday morning Hollister was again on the line with Mason. 'I am inviting you,' he said, 'to a Press conference aboard the yacht of Otto Olney. It is taking place at two o'clock this afternoon at the Penguin Yacht Club. You are invited to be present and to stay for cocktails – two to five.'

'What about filing the suit?' Mason asked.

'We're filing the suit at one o'clock this afternoon,' Hollister said. 'Our client is very much annoyed over the statement attributed to Mr Durant, and your affidavit by Maxine Lindsay covers the situation perfectly. We are asking damages in an amount of twenty-five thousand dollars. Mr Olney places a very high valuation on this particular picture and feels that the statements made by Durant not only reflect on the value of the picture, but on his judgement as a businessman. Furthermore, our client has gone all the way and has alleged in his complaint that the statements were made deliberately and with malice, and has asked for another twenty-five thousand as punitive or exemplary damages.'

'I'll be glad to be present,' Mason said. 'I take it I may bring my secretary, Miss Street?'

'Certainly.'

'We'll be there. I'm glad you're going ahead with the suit.'

'We don't like to play cat's-paw for other people,' Hollister said tartly. 'Of course the *real* cause of action is one that Rankin has against Durant.'

'I take it,' Mason said, 'Olney is able to compensate you for your services in the matter.'

'Quite able,' Hollister said.

'All right,' Mason told him, 'we didn't bring you in as a cat's paw, we handed you a piece of legal business. I take it I'll meet *you* at two o'clock?'

'I'll be there,' Hollister said.

'I'll look forward to meeting you then.'

The lawyer hung up and turned to Della Street who had been monitoring the conversation.

'To thunder with all this business of sitting in a musty old office, Della, browsing through the files of antiquity in order to find out the course of legal reasoning which has actuated judges in determining litigation. Let's leave the office at one, drive leisurely down to the Penguin Yacht Club, board the palatial yacht of Otto Olney, look at the picture in question, and imbibe several cocktails; after which we can have dinner and perhaps engage in a little dancing, just by way of exercise.'

'I take it,' she said, 'that my presence is necessary as a part of the business in hand.'

'Oh, quite necessary,' Mason said. 'I wouldn't think of being there without you.'

'Under those circumstances,' she observed demurely, 'it would seem only right that I should call the client who has the three o'clock appointment with you and tell him that a matter of urgent business has necessitated postponing the appointment.'

'Who is it, Della?'

'The man who wanted to see you about the appeal in that case of his brother – the one where the brother's attorney failed to object on the alleged misconduct of the prosecutor.'

'Oh, yes,' Mason said, 'I remember now. That is an interesting case but there's no great hurry about it. Ring him up and tell him that I'll see him at twelve-thirty instead of at three, or he can have the appointment tomorrow. Take a look at the appointment book and see if you can fit him in, but we definitely can't let anything interfere with appraising the art work of Phellipe Feteet. As a matter of fact, the description of the man's technique interests me a lot.'

Della Street smiled as Mason picked up a pile of urgent mail she had stacked on a corner of his desk. 'Nothing,' she observed, 'leads you to tackle routine matters with greater energy or more enthusiasm than the prospect of getting away from the office and running head-on into adventure.'

Mason weighed the accusation for a moment, then gleefully acknowledged the accuracy of her observation. 'We need a little adventure, Della. Let's get through with this damned bunch of routine stuff, then go have a ball.'

With which, the lawyer plunged into the pile of mail.

At ten minutes to one, Mason and Della Street entered the lawyer's car, stopped briefly at a roadside drive-in for lunch, then went on down to the Penguin Yacht Club, made inquiries as to the location of Otto Olney's yacht and shortly thereafter were escorted aboard a trim craft which looked like a miniature ocean liner.

A tall, tired-looking individual in his late forties, wearing a yachting cap, a blue coat and white trousers, came forward to greet them. 'I'm Olney,' he said, glancing at Perry Mason, then letting his eyes shift approvingly to Della Street.

'Perry Mason,' the lawyer told him, 'and this is Miss Street, my confidential secretary.'

'How do you do, how do you do?' Olney said, shaking hands. 'You're a little early. Would you care to step in and make yourselves comfortable? Perhaps a drink?'

'We've just eaten,' Mason said. 'It's a little early for a drink but I'd like to look at the painting. I had some conversations with your attorneys about the case.'

'Yes, yes, I know. Come in and take a look.'

Olney led the way into a luxuriously furnished main saloon, dominated artistically by a painting showing women stripped to the waist grouped under the shade of a tree while just behind them in vivid sunlight naked children romped against a background of riotous colour.

'The idea of saying *that* picture's a fake!' Olney exclaimed. 'That's up in the headhunters' country, back of Baguio, and Phellipe Feteet is the only artist who was ever able to get the spirit of the thing. Just look at the depth in that picture! Look at the texture of the skin on those women! Look at the expressions on their faces, and then look at that sunlight. You can just see it beating down. You want to get back into the shelter of the shade of a tree and sit with the women.'

Mason, startled, said, 'Why, that's one of the most unusual paintings I've ever seen!'

'Thank you, thank you, thank you!' Olney exclaimed. 'I'm a fan of Feteet's. The guy had something no one else ever has developed and I'd like to buy more of his paintings if I could get hold of them at anything like a reasonable price. I'm satisfied they're going to be tremendously valuable someday.'

'I should certainly think so,' Mason said. 'Those women –

the colours – the background – there's so much depth to the picture.'

'You can get depth if you can get a shaded foreground with a sunlit background,' Olney said, 'but very few people are able to achieve it. Most of the pictures showing sunlight are pale, insipid things with a sort of pastel sunlight. It looks as though you were looking at a coloured photograph taken on a hazy day.

'But Feteet had the knack of making the shade cool and comfortable and having it dominate the foreground so that the vivid colouring of the background suggests a type of sunlight that— Ah, here's Miss Kenner. I want you to meet her.'

Olney went forward to shake hands with a serious-eyed, quite good-looking woman in her mid-thirties who gave him her hand and said casually, 'Hi, Otto. What is it *this* time?'

'This time,' Olney said, 'you are going to get a surprise. But I don't want to announce it until some of the other people get here. Ah, here's Hollister now.'

Hollister, a bundle of dynamic energy, closely knit, quick-moving, briefcase in hand, boarded the yacht and was introduced to Mason and Della Street. Then after a moment a group of newspaper reporters appeared, accompanied by photographers with Press cameras, and last, Lattimer Rankin came stalking majestically across the landing and aboard the yacht.

'Where's Maxine?' Olney asked.

'I thought it better for her not to come,' Hollister said. 'We have her affidavit and there's no use having her interviewed by the Press when we can use her affidavit, which speaks for itself.'

For a moment there was a flicker of disappointment on Olney's face. Then he said curtly, 'Okay, you're the attorney.'

Olney was busy for a while greeting newspaper reporters. Then, seeing that the gathering was complete, he said, 'Ladies and gentlemen, we are going to have cocktails and then I am going to tell you the reason for this gathering.'

One of the newspaper reporters said, 'Look, Olney, we know the reason for the gathering. Your attorney has filed suit about this painting by Feteet. Now, cocktails are all right but we want to get a story to the papers and we might as well get the story *before* we have the cocktails.'

One of the photographers said, 'If you'll just stand up in front of the painting, Mr Olney . . .'

Lattimer Rankin stepped forward. 'Now, just a minute,' he said, 'I want to have this thing done right. I want—'

'Now, wait a minute, who are you?' one of the reporters interrupted.

Another one said, 'He's the guy that sold the picture in the first place.'

'Okay, okay, get up in front of the picture. You can stand with Olney.'

'Now, just a minute,' Corliss Kenner said. 'I don't want to be the only expert interviewed on this matter. I have another expert coming. I don't know why he wasn't invited in place of me. He's the greatest expert on this particular type of art there is in the country. I was surprised to find he hadn't been invited earlier.'

She turned to look at Olney. 'I am referring to George Lathan Howell. I took the liberty of inviting him on my own responsibility, Otto. I hope you don't mind. There are reasons why I felt it advisable. He should be here any minute.'

Hollister said, 'Now hold on. This is a lawsuit and I want to have something to say about how it's handled. The witnesses—'

'Hello, everybody,' a voice said. 'Looks as though I'm a little late.'

'Here's Howell now,' Corliss Kenner said, relief in her voice.

Mason regarded the thirty-five-year-old brown-eyed, bronzed individual who entered the saloon with a light, springy step and the easy affability of one who is assured of his welcome anywhere.

'*Now* we can go ahead,' Corliss said.

Otto Olney said, 'As the reporters know, and most of you people are now entitled to know, an accusation has been made that this painting by Phellipe Feteet is a forgery.'

'Oh, for God's sake!' Howell exclaimed.

Rankin said, 'The authenticity of that painting stands out

like a sore thumb. No other painter could get that effective brilliance, that pigmentation, that—'

'Now, hold everything,' Olney said, 'I want to serve some cocktails. Let's get these pictures taken. You boys want photographs and you shall have them. Come on now, we'll get up in front of the painting. You, Hollister, come up here. Rankin, you should be here and Corliss, we'll want you. And, of course, Howell.'

'Not I,' said Hollister. 'I don't want to be put in the position of trying a lawsuit in the newspapers. I don't think I'd better be in that photograph, and as far as Mr Howell is concerned—'

'Howell is the greatest living expert on this type of art,' Otto Olney said. 'I'm glad he's here.'

One of the reporters said, 'All right, get up in front of the painting. Now, don't look as though you're having your picture taken. Don't look at the camera. Be looking at the painting. You'll have to get in fairly close – we don't want pictures of the backs of your heads. You can keep your profiles to the camera.'

The photographers quickly arranged the group. Flash bulbs flared, camera backs clicked at the slides on film holders were put in and withdrawn.

'Okay,' one reporter said, 'we've got the pictures. Now let's have the rest of the story.'

Olney said, 'Collin M. Durant, a self-styled art expert, a man who claims to be a dealer, has seen fit to challenge the authenticity of this picture. He has stated that it's not a genuine Feteet.'

'Good Lord,' Corliss Kenner said, 'can you imagine anyone who knows anything about art making a statement like that!'

Olney said, 'Now, I'd like to have Mr Howell make a statement—'

Hollister interrupted. 'We have these art experts here. Now, if we get them photographed we're going to have to put them on the witness-stand. Otherwise, it will give the impression that one of our witnesses backed down.'

'Well, nobody's backing down,' Howell said, laughing. 'You don't need to make a close examination of this canvas to know who did it. I think any reputable art expert in the country could look at that canvas clear across a museum and give the name of the painter and the approximate date of the painting. This was done somewhere between thirty-three and thirty-five in the period of Feteet's painting when he was beginning to uncover a new technique. If the man had lived he might well have revolutionized contemporary painting.

'The only reason he didn't establish a school is that nobody else has been able to duplicate his effect.'

'I think it's something in the pigmentation,' Corliss Kenner said.

Howell nodded. 'There's no question about that. He had some secret of mixing his paints. The results show that. Look at the skin on the shoulders of these women under the tree. The smooth texture, the sheen – someone has claimed that he put a little coconut oil in his paints.'

'Well, that isn't it,' Corliss Kenner said. 'Coconut oil won't work.'

'You tried it?' Howell asked.

She hesitated, then smiled and said, 'I experimented a bit. I'd like to find out just what his secret was. I guess every art expert would.'

Men in white coats entered the saloon carrying silver trays on which were glasses, ice, and bottles.

Otto Olney said, 'We have Scotch and soda. We have bourbon and the conventional mixers. We have Manhattans. We have Old Fashioneds and Martinis already mixed. We're opening up a bar at the far end and—'

One of the reporters said, 'How much did this yacht set you back, Olney?'

'I have more than three hundred thousand in it,' Olney said quietly.

'How do you keep it up? Do you write it off?'

'It is used for entertaining in a business way.'

'It is true you keep all your paintings here?' the reporter asked.

'I keep many of them, yes,' Olney said.

'Why?'

There was a silence. Then Olney said stiffly, 'I find it convenient and I like to have them near me. I spend a good deal of my time on the yacht.'

Hollister said to Mason, 'He and his wife don't have the same tastes. She doesn't like art and doesn't like the art crowd. He lives on the yacht a great deal of the time.'

'Divorce?' Mason asked.

'There won't be any.'

A waiter appeared at Mason's elbow. 'Mr Olney would like to know your pleasure.'

Mason glanced at Della Street.

'Scotch and soda,' she said.

Mason nodded. 'Make it two.'

'Yes, sir.'

Hollister said, 'It's hard to keep these things from getting out of hand. I think it's a good idea to have a story but I don't want to be accused of using publicity to create a prejudicial atmosphere in a lawsuit. I don't think that's ethical.'

'It's frowned upon,' Mason said dryly.

Howell, moving over to the painting, took a magnifying glass from his pocket, examined the canvas carefully.

Mason, accepting the Scotch and soda from the waiter, moved over to stand by Howell's side.

'Well?' he asked.

'No doubt of it on earth,' Howell said, 'but I'm just making sure so that some *smart* lawyer can't cross-examine me and—

'Now, wait a minute,' Howell went on hurriedly, 'I didn't mean that personally, Mr Mason. You know there are lawyers and lawyers.'

'Just as there are art dealers and art dealers,' Mason said, laughing.

'Exactly,' Howell said. 'I didn't know anything about this until Corliss called me. I don't know how in the world any art dealer could have doubted the authenticity of this canvas ... Tell you what, Mason, this is going to be a great thing for the Phellipe Feteets that are in existence. There are only about two dozen of them. Personally, I'd add three to five thousand dollars to the price of each one just on the strength of this publicity, and that's a conservative estimate.

'If you ever get a chance to pick up a Feteet at anything under fifteen thousand dollars, grab it as an investment.'

'Think they're going up?' Mason asked.

'I *know* they're going up,' Howell said. 'How did all this start, anyway?'

'As I understand it,' Mason said, 'although I am not a attorney of record, at a gathering here a dealer by the name of Durant—'

'I know him,' Howell interposed, 'sort of an unscrupulous publicity hound. Go on.'

'Expressed an opinion in a conversation that the picture was spurious.'

'Tell Olney that?' Howell asked.

'No,' Mason said, 'a young artist named Maxine Lindsay was the one to whom the statement was made.'

Howell's face froze into immobility. 'I see,' he said, without expression.

'And,' Mason went on, 'I believe she repeated what had been said to Mr Rankin, the dealer who sold Olney the picture. Rankin communicated with Olney and quite naturally Olney was furious. He feels that Durant's opinion, if permitted to stand unchallenged, will affect the value of the painting.'

'We'll, there's one thing certain,' Howell said, 'nobody in his right mind is going to challenge the authenticity of *that* painting.'

Mason turned back to Della Street, touched the rim of his glass to hers. 'Here's looking at you,' he said.

'Right back at you,' she told him. 'How long do we stay? There's always the chance this might become a brawl.'

'We stay just long enough to size up the situation,' Mason said.

A flash bulb flared. A photographer said, 'Hope you don't have any objections, Mr Mason, but you and your secretary, standing shoulder to shoulder looking in each other's eyes, makes a better story for *my* paper than this story about the painting that all the other fellows are going to have. What's your interest in this?'

'Just curiosity,' Mason said. 'I was invited and thought I'd look in to see how the other half lives.'

'I get you,' the reporter said, laughing. 'Slumming, eh?'

Mason turned to Della Street with a smile.

'Let's go shake hands with our host and be on our way.'

'Back to the office?' Della Street asked with a smile.

'Don't be silly!' Mason said. 'We can find a lot better things to do than that. Let's go down to Marineland – you can telephone Gertie that we won't be back. Tell her to get in touch with Paul Drake at the Drake Detective Agency in case anything breaks that needs us. You can tell her I'll give Paul a ring before we finish up for the evening ... and we can have dinner and a few dances at the Robbers' Roost.'

Della Street extended her arm. 'Twist,' she said.

CHAPTER FIVE

Mason and Della Street were finishing their after-dinner coffee when the waiter placed a newspaper clipping in front of the attorney.

'I suppose you've seen it, Mr Mason,' he said. '*We're* very proud of it.'

Mason looked at the clipping, one of the syndicated gossip columns of goings-on about town.

'No, I hadn't seen it,' he said.

Della Street leaned forward, and Mason held the clipping so they could both read.

Dining and dancing at the Robbers' Roost is quite frequently on the agenda these nights for Perry Mason, famous criminal lawyer whose trials are usually filled with legal fireworks. The night spot is doing brisk business thanks to the people who want to take a look at the well-known attorney and his deep-dish secretary – who is said to shadow him at work and at play, by the way.

Mason handed the clipping back to the waiter with a smile. 'I hadn't seen it,' he said.

'Well,' Della said, as the waiter vanished, 'I suppose that means the end of another good eating place.'

'For dinner dancing,' Mason said, 'you can't beat it. But

40

once the word gets around that I can be found here, heaven knows how many pests will cut in on us.'

'Unless I am greatly mistaken,' Della Street said, 'and as a good secretary I seldom make a mistake in such matters, one of these pests is bearing down upon us right now. He is approaching the table with a singleness of purpose indicating a desire either to secure legal advice without being billed for it, or to be able to mention casually, "As I was having a drink with Perry Mason last night in the Robbers' Roost, he said to me . . ."'

She broke off as the man in question came within earshot, a small boned, wiry individual in his late thirties; nervous, intense, quick-moving.

'Mr Mason?' he said.

Mason regarded the man coldly. 'Yes?'

'You don't know me and I'm sorry I have to approach you in this manner but it's a matter of great urgency.'

'To you or me?' Massn asked.

The man ignored the remark. 'I'm Collin Durant,' he said. 'I'm an art dealer and critic. The newspapers have been pestering me over some smear that Otto Olney dished out this afternoon. I understand you're in on it.'

'Your understanding is incorrect,' Mason said. 'I am not "*in*" on any "*smear*" being "*dished out*" by Otto Olney.'

'I understand he's suing me, claiming that I've cheapened his paintings, questioned his judgement and branded one of his paintings as spurious.'

'As to that,' Mason said, 'you'll have to talk with Mr Olney. I'm not an attorney of record in any such case and have no intention of becoming one.'

'But you were there this afternoon. The newspaper photographs show you and your secretary – I take it this is Miss Street who is with you tonight?'

Mason said, 'I attended a Press conference given by Otto Olney on his yacht this afternoon. I gave no interview to the Press and I don't care to be interviewed now.'

Durant reached over to an adjoining table, whipped a vacant chair around, seated himself, said, 'All right, now I want you to hear my side of it.'

Mason said, 'I have no desire whatever to hear your side of

it. I am not in a position to treat anything you may say as confidential, nor do I have any business which I care to discuss with you.'

'This is something *I'm* going to discuss with *you*,' Durant said.

'In the first place, I don't know what Olney is talking about. I was never called on by him to express any opinion in regard to any of his paintings. I was a guest on his yacht about a week ago.

'Naturally, being a dealer, I looked over his collection of paintings with an appraising eye but I didn't make any careful inspection because there was no reason for me to do so.

'The man did have a Phellipe Feteet, or what passed for one. I didn't examine it. I only glanced at it casually. I understand he paid some thirty-five hundred dollars for it. It is a painting of which he is very proud. I never said it was a forgery. I would have to examine it with great care to make certain. I will say, however, there were some things about the painting that I would want to study carefully if I were to be called upon to express an opinion.'

Mason said, 'I'm not asking you to make any statement. I'm not interested in your version of the case and I didn't ask you to sit down.'

'All right,' Durant said, 'let's put it this way. I invited myself to sit down and since the newspapers have dignified Olney's suit by having you and your secretary listed among those present at the Press conference, I'm going to tell you that I'm not going to stand for all this.

'I understand that the only person who says I expressed an opinion is a former model who I have reason to believe is anxious to secure a lot of cheap publicity. Or perhaps I should express it the other way: who is anxious to secure a lot of publicity cheap.

'I would like very much to find out whether this person is the one who is back of all this uproar. I never told her or anyone else anything about the painting, except that I think I told this young woman that if anyone asked me to give an opinion on the painting, I would want to examine it most carefully. That's what I would have to do before I could express an opinion on *any* painting.

'I'm not going to let this publicity seeker parley a statement like that into a bid for newspaper notoriety.'

'I can't tell you anything,' Mason said, 'and I have no desire to discuss the matter.'

'Don't discuss it if you don't want to, you can just listen,' Durant said.

'And I have no desire to listen,' Mason said, pushing back his chair. 'I'm trying to relax,' he went on, 'from the day's work. I am dining socially. I don't care to discuss any business at this time and I have nothing to discuss with you.'

The lawyer got to his feet.

'I'm just telling you,' Durant said, 'that any time any cheap trollop thinks she's going to bounce her curves off *my* reputation as an art dealer in order to feather her own nest, she has a surprise coming.'

Mason said, 'I've tried to be courteous about this, Durant. I've told you repeatedly I don't care to discuss anything with you. Now, you can get up out of that chair and start moving or *you've* got a surprise coming.'

Durant looked at the angry lawyer, shrugged his shoulders, got to his feet, said, 'And the same thing goes for you, Mr Mason. I have a business reputation and I'm not going to have it cheapened by you or anyone else.'

Mason walked over, picked up the chair Durant had been sitting in, replaced it at the adjoining table, turned his back on Durant and again seated himself opposite Della Street.

Durant walked away after a moment's hesitation.

Della Street reached across to put her hand over that of Perry Mason. Her fingers strong, steady, capable, gave his hand a reassuring squeeze.

'Don't look after him like that, Chief,' she said. 'If looks could kill, you'd be your own defendant in a murder case.'

Mason moved his eyes back to Della Street's face and then his own face softened into a smile. 'Thanks, Della,' he said, 'I was actually contemplating justifiable homicide. I don't know exactly why he irritated me so much.

'Of course, I hate to have my evening interfered with by people who want to take short cuts on getting legal advice. I don't like table-hoppers, I don't like name-droppers.'

'And,' Della Street said, 'you don't like art experts by the name of Collin Durant.'

'Period,' Mason said.

'Well,' Della Street told him, 'being virtually assured that you are now going to leave this place and not return until the notoriety connected with that gossip column has abated somewhat, do you think it would be a good plan for me to call the Drake Detective Agency and see what Paul knows, if anything?'

'It might be a very good plan,' Mason said, 'to keep in touch with him.'

The lawyer reached in his pocket.

'I have a whole purseful of dimes,' Della Street said. 'Drink your coffee and relax. I'll be back in a moment with all the dirt from Paul.'

Della Street vanished in the direction of the telephone booth. Mason poured another cup of coffee, settled back and let the stiffness and tension flow out of his muscles as he contemplated the couples dancing, the people eating.

Della Street was back in a few minutes.

'What's cooking?' Mason asked.

'Nothing on the front burner,' she said, 'and nothing in the oven. But something is simmering on the back burner.'

'Such as what?'

'Maxine Lindsay.'

'What about her?'

'She called just a few minutes ago and insisted that she had to speak to you tonight, that she *must* get in touch with you.'

'What did Drake say?'

'He told her he couldn't reach you, that you'd probably call in during the evening. Then Maxine said while she wanted to reach you she knew how busy you were and it might not be necessary to bother you if she could just get in touch with your secretary, Della Street.'

'Did Paul give her your phone number?'

'That's right.'

'That means you'll probably get a call late tonight.'

'That's all right, it won't bother me any. What will I tell her?'

'Just see what she has in mind and tell her to stay put. Call her attention to the fact that I have an affidavit from her so she can't change her testimony.'

Della Street nodded.

Mason said, 'You know, Della, the law schools teach law. No one teaches anything about the facts to which the law is applied, or what to do about those facts. Yet when a young lawyer starts practising law he finds that his problems for the most part don't deal with law but deal with proof. In other words, they deal with facts.

'Now, let's take *this* case for instance. Rankin was all steamed up. He wanted to file suit. He wanted to get his name in the paper. He wanted to put his own professional reputation out on the block and he had a perfect legal right to do so. If I had let him walk into that trap, however, he'd have been hung, drawn, and quartered in the market-place Everyone would have remembered him as the art dealer who had been accused by another art dealer of peddling a phoney painting.

'Now, however, the shoe is on the other foot. Durant is on the defensive, Rankin is sitting pretty, and the ultimate result will be to enhance Rankin's reputation – but we're still up against facts.'

'Such as what?' Della Street asked.

'First,' Mason said, 'we have to prove that the Phellipe Feteet Rankin sold Otto Olney is genuine.'

'That seems to have been taken care of all right,' she said.

Mason nodded.

'The next thing,' Mason said, 'is to *prove* that Durant said the picture was spurious. We have a witness for that end of it all tied up, but apparently that's where Durant is going to make his fight.'

'Well,' Della Street said, 'Maxine was most definite in her statement – she can't back up on her testimony now. I really made an affidavit. I tied her up, up one side and down the other.'

'That's what's worrying me,' Mason said. 'If anything should happen to Maxine, we couldn't use her affidavit as testimony. The only purpose of the affidavit is to keep her in line, to hold it over her head in case she should start getting vague and changing her testimony.'

'She won't do that,' Della Street said reassuringly.

'And there's one other thing,' Mason said.

'What?'

'Suppose she should marry Collin Durant?'

'Heaven forbid!'

'But just suppose she should,' Mason said.

'Well, there's no use worrying about it,' Della Street told him.

'I don't know,' Mason said. 'There's something fishy about this whole business. The lawyer in me is beginning to wave red danger signals all up and down the track.'

She said, 'The lawyer in you makes you so sceptical that you're always looking for the joker in the deck.'

'I am, for a fact,' Mason admitted, 'but there's something about the way Durant is acting that bothers me.'

'What is it?'

'I'll be darned if I know,' Mason said. 'It's in his manner – his attitude – something about the way he approached us. Did you ever hear of the famous jewellery bunco game that put so many jewellers out of business?'

'No,' Della said, her voice showing her interest.

Mason said, 'A personable young man goes into a jewellery store at four-thirty Friday afternoon after the banks have closed. He tells a very plausible story. He picks the leading jeweller in a small town. He wants to get a very fine diamond as an engagement ring. He is going to propose that night. He's happy and impulsive and he has the best of credit references and the jeweller finally sells him a fifteen-hundred-dollar diamond ring and takes the man's cheque drawn on a city bank.'

'Then what?' Della Street asked. 'You mean the cheque is no good?'

'No, no,' Mason said. 'The cheque is as good as gold. That's the catch in the thing.'

'I don't get it,' Della Street said.

'The next day,' Mason said, 'the fellow goes to a pawn-shop and wants to pawn the ring for two hundred dollars. The ring is worth about seven hundred and fifty wholesale. The pawn-broker becomes suspicious and notifies the police. The police come and interview the man and ask him where he got the ring and he tells them that he bought it at the jewellery store. So they check with the jeweller and the jeweller says, "Sure

46

enough. The fellow bought the ring and paid for it with a cheque," but of course he's now completely satisfied he's the victim of a bad-cheque artist and tells the police to hold the fellow as a swindler.

'The police hold him until Monday morning when the jeweller can get in touch with the city bank and present the cheque. Then, to his consternation, he finds the cheque is good as gold.

'The young man tells a story of having purchased the ring, of having proposed to the woman of his choice only to be given a flat rebuff, so he has no use for the ring and every time he looks at it he becomes nauseated with thoughts of his frustrated love affair.

'He says he was too proud to go back to the jeweller and admit to him that he had been turned down. He wanted to get rid of the ring and was willing to take anything he could get on it, so he went to this pawnshop and asked if they'd give him two hundred dollars for the ring.

'Then in order to make the thing absolutely ironclad he gives the name of the girl to whom he had proposed. The police interview the girl and she confirms his story in every detail. He had been courting her and she had liked him but didn't consider he was really in love with her. She thought he was just escorting her around and thought it was just a friendship. So when the fellow came to her with the diamond ring and proposed, he had been drinking a little bit and, what with one thing and another, she decided he wasn't the sort of person she wanted as a husband and turned him down flat.

'So the fellow is angry over his arrest and goes to a lawyer and files suit for a hundred and fifty thousand dollars' damages against the jeweller who had him arrested and held in jail over the weekend. He claims his reputation has been damaged and he's going to insist on collecting damages for false arrest.'

'Does he do it?' Della Street asked.

'No, he doesn't do it,' Mason said. 'That's the pay-off. He offers to let the jeweller off the hook if the jeweller will let him keep the diamond ring and give him anywhere from two to fifteen thousand dollars in cash, depending on how frightened the jeweller is.

'So the guy makes his settlement and doesn't have anything

to do until next Friday when he pulls the same gag on another country jeweller somewhere, always picking one who's reasonably prosperous, who's afraid of litigation and who simply couldn't stand to have a big judgement outstanding.'

'But surely there isn't anything like that in this case,' Della Street said.

'I don't know,' Mason said. 'There's something about the whole thing that bothers me. All the time that man, Durant, was talking to me I had the idea he was putting on an act. He was ... well, he wasn't really trying to accomplish anything, he was being deliberately obnoxious and he was laying the foundation for some kind of a racket. He wasn't sincere.'

'How can you tell?' Della Street asked.

'I'm darned if I know,' Mason said, 'but it's something that any lawyer can tell after he's cross-examined enough witnesses. You listen to a man's story, you watch his actions, his mannerisms, you listen to his voice, you watch his facial expressions and – well, you just *know*, that's all.

'It's something that's difficult to describe, but you've seen motion pictures where the director has tried to milk too much out of a situation, where he's had the actors over-acting just a little, and all of a sudden you get the realization that the whole thing is phoney, that it's just a lot of actors mugging in front of a camera.

'On the other hand, you see some movies where the actors are doing a good job, the director is after the right effect, and you get the illusion of reality. It's as though you were looking through a window at real genuine action that is taking place before your eyes.'

'Well, of course,' Della Street said, 'I've had *that* experience. Unfortunately it isn't as frequent as I'd like.'

'I know,' Mason said. 'That's because different people have a different threshold of credulity. The average person looks at action which has been photographed and thinks the action is real. A lawyer or someone who has been working with a lawyer, like you, becomes more sceptical, and the faintest overacting, the faintest attempt to milk a situation past a critical point and you suddenly revolt. The subconscious mind refuses to accept the story, the conscious mind enters the picture with the realization that the whole thing is phoney. They're suddenly just a bunch of actors and actresses reciting a script with background scenery that was cooked up in a studio and there isn't the faintest illusion of reality – there's nothing except irritation and annoyance with yourself for wasting perfectly good time sitting there watching a lousy show.'

'And you think Durant put on a lousy show?' Della Street asked.

Mason said, 'He didn't impress me as putting on the right kind of an act as far as sincerity was concerned. He was trying to accomplish something when he was talking to me. He was acting and it wasn't an act that went across.'

'But with Maxine's affidavit she can't back out on her testimony,' Della Street said.

'She could of course vanish,' Mason said. 'Suppose Otto Olney gets ready to try his lawsuit and can't find Maxine. Suppose Durant indignantly denies that he ever said the Feteet was spurious. Suppose he claims that Olney's suit has discredited him as an expert, that the resulting publicity has irreparably damaged him – damn it, Della, I've got a feeling, an intuitive feeling predicated on that guy's phoney performance, that I've led with my chin somewhere along the line.'

'*You* haven't,' Della Street said.

'The hell I haven't,' Mason said. 'I'm the one that suggested to Rankin that he get Olney to file suit. I'm the one that told Olney's attorneys about how it should be handled.

'Olney is vulnerable to the extent that every rich man is vulnerable. A case comes up in front of a jury. Durant is the young, ambitious art dealer trying to get ahead. He makes a pathetic picture in front of a jury. Olney, the big contractor, filed suit against Durant, without first calling on Durant and giving him an opportunity to explain. The first thing Durant knew, out of a clear sky he sees himself blasted in the Press as a phoney, a man who has branded a painting as spurious. Actually, he claims, he never said any such thing, and if Otto Olney had taken the trouble to investigate instead of breaking into the front page of the newspapers, he would have learned that the whole thing was a mistake on the part of the woman he was relying on as a witness.'

'Then, do you think Maxine is in on it?' Della Street asked.

'I don't know,' Mason said, 'but I'm going to find out ...
You know, that's the tragic part of those cases where the jewellers were sued for putting a man in jail over the weekend.
They just didn't have guts enough to fight and to dig into the
guy's past, to check on the girl and find out all about her ...
Come on, Della, we're going up to Drake's office and see that
he has a sleepless night. By this time tomorrow we're going to
know all there is to know about the background of Maxine
Lindsay and all we can find out about Collin M. Durant.'

'All on the strength of the fact that you didn't like Durant?'
Della Street asked.

'All on the strength of the fact that Durant impresses me as
a phoney,' Mason said, 'and if Otto Olney with his money has
been trapped into a situation of this sort, I intend to beat
everybody to the punch. I want to get all the ammunition I
need to do a little shooting of my own.'

'And if it turns out to be a false alarm?' Della asked.

'Then we've given Paul Drake a good job,' Mason said, 'and
have at least laid the foundation for me to get a good night's
sleep. I tell you, Della, I've cross-examined too many witnesses to be taken in by a phoney act of the kind Durant tried,
and Durant *was* putting on an act; that much I'll stake money
on. We're going up to Drake's office and start the ball rolling.'

CHAPTER SIX

Mason and Della Street left the elevator just as the door of the
entrance office to the Drake Detective Agency opened and
Paul Drake emerged.

'Well, hello, you two,' Drake said. 'Headed for your office
for a spot of night work? I didn't think you were going to be
up.'

'We're headed for *your* office,' Mason said, 'and we've got a
lot of night work for you.'

'Oh, no!' Drake moaned. 'This was the night I was going to
catch that show I've been trying to see for so long. I've got a

line out on your girlfriend, Maxine. I've got a choice ticket and—'

'And you're turning it in,' Mason said. 'Come on back, Paul.'

'What's the trouble?' Drake said. 'Another murder?'

'Hell, no,' Mason told him. 'I wish it were another murder. Those things are simple. This is something I'm involved in.'

Drake glanced inquiringly at Della Street.

'He's taken a button and sewn a vest on it,' Della Street said, 'but I guess you're going to have to go to work.'

'All right,' Drake said, 'come on in. Incidentally, I left a note for you. As I told Della on the phone, your Maxine has been calling. She left a number. I said I didn't think you'd be in at all tonight. Here's the number. Want to call her? I gave her Della's number. Calling her now would save having Della disturbed later.'

Mason shook his head. 'Later, not now. I want to think things over for a few minutes – want to talk them over.'

Drake held the door open for them, said to the girl at the switchboard, 'Here's a theatre ticket. Give it to one of the operatives to surrender for cash, to peddle, or he can see the show.'

Drake opened the wicket gate which led to the long runway with little offices opening on each side, and Della Street led the way down the familiar alleyway to Drake's office.

Drake seated Della Street, indicated a chair for Mason, then seated himself behind the desk on which there were several telephones.

Mason said, 'Damn it, Paul, I wish you'd get a bigger office! There isn't room for me to pace and I can't think without pacing.'

Drake grinned. 'You just tell me your troubles, Perry, and then go down to your office and start pacing while you plan how you're going to get enough money out of your clients to pay my bill, because I'm adding the price of a scalper's theatre ticket to my services tonight, as general overhead.'

Mason said, 'The hell of it is, Paul, Della Street is right. I've taken a button and sewn a vest on it – but the vest matches the button.'

'Well?' Drake asked.

'The button is real,' Mason said, 'and for the life of me I can't see how it fits into the picture unless it goes on a vest.'

'All right, tell me about the vest,' Drake said.

Mason said. 'It's like the old phoney jewellery store bad-cheque racket, Paul, where the con man traps the jeweller into ordering his arrest over the weekend.'

'Who's the victim?'

'Otto Olney.'

'Not on that painting deal,' Drake said. 'I read about that in the evening papers.'

'It's that painting deal,' Mason said.

'What's the matter, Perry, is the painting phoney?'

'No, the painting is absolutely genuine.'

'Well, then what does anyone have to worry about?'

'I'm not certain Olney can prove that Durant said it wasn't genuine.'

'For heaven's sake, didn't Olney tie that up before he started suit?' Drake asked. 'He has a good firm of attorneys. I happen to know them, Warton, Warton, Cosgrove, and Hollister.'

'Sure, they're good,' Mason said, 'and I'm the one that sewed up that angle for them. I had Della take an affidavit from this girl, Maxine Lindsay, to whom Durant made the statement.'

'You have the affidavit?'

'That's right.'

'Well, what's wrong?' Drake asked.

'I have an idea Maxine is planning to run out on us.'

'Well, how about getting in touch with her right now?' Drake asked. 'We can call her at the number she left.'

'Not *right* now,' Mason said. 'I'm going to see her, and I'd like to find out something about her before we see her.'

'Tell me the rest of it,' Drake said.

'Now here's what happened. Durant got in touch with me tonight and put on an act. It was an act. I'm absolutely positive of that.'

'How do you know?' Drake asked.

There was a moment's silence.

Drake turned to Della Street. 'Did he trap him in some contradictory statement, Della?'

She shook her head and said, 'Instinct.'

Drake grinned.

'Don't grin,' Mason said. 'I've cross-examined enough witnesses so I can tell when a man's putting on an act. Durant got in touch with me and put on an act. It was something he'd carefully rehearsed. It was something that was an essential step in the particular type of bunco game the guy is pulling.

'Now then, if my hunch is correct, Maxine is calling me to tell me that something has happened that she can't explain over the telephone, that she is leaving; that it's an emergency in her personal life; that she'll get in touch with me so I can call on her. to testify when the proper time comes. Then she'll disappear.'

'And you won't be able to find her?'

'And I won't be able to find her,' Mason said. 'No one will be able to find her. Durant will be screaming his head off that his reputation has been damaged, his integrity as an art dealer has been assailed, his judgement has been questioned and all the rest of it, and will demand an immediate trial. Olney will find his witness is missing.

'Olney can prove that the painting is genuine, all right. There won't be any question of that. But he won't be able to prove that Durant said it *wasn't* genuine.'

'So then Durant's lawyers will suggest Olney decorate the mahogany in order to avoid a suit of slander?' Drake asked.

Mason nodded.

'So what do we do?' Drake asked.

Mason said, 'Maxine wants to get in touch with me. Now, I'm going to manipulate things so that she has to get in touch with me at a certain place. That place will be Della Street's apartment house. That's a good place to begin because she'll have to come there in a cab or in a car. She'll either come alone or she'll come with someone. She'll probably come in her own car and alone.

'You can have half a dozen men spotted around the neighbourhood. You can pick up her trail, and once you pick it up I don't want you to drop it.

'What's more, I want you to keep digging into the past of Maxine Lindsay. I want to find out all you can find out about her, and at the same time you can dig into the background of

53

Collin Durant. Durant won't have anything very flagrant in his background because he wouldn't be in a position to stick his reputation on the line unless anything that was detrimental was pretty well covered up. The weak link in the chain will be Maxine.'

Drake said, 'That's going to cost a lot of money.'

'I know it's going to cost a lot of money,' Mason said. 'It's going to cost a lot of money no matter which way the cat jumps. I have a definite feeling there's something phoney about this whole thing. You can imagine the position I'll be in if the word gets around that Perry Mason was played for a sucker.'

'Where do you fit into the picture?'

'I fit into the picture because Lattimer Rankin, the dealer who sold Otto Olney the picture in the first place, was the one who was primarily damaged by Collin Durant's sneering remark.'

'And how did he know about it?'

'Maxine Lindsay told him.'

'And why did she tell him?'

'Because he's been befriending her. She's been trying to get started as a photographic portrait painter and Rankin had been helping her. She was grateful to him and—'

'Oh-oh,' Drake said, 'I begin to get the picture. It does look a little fishy.'

'Everything is there, every element,' Mason said. 'Confidentially, Paul, Rankin came to me and wanted me to file suit against Durant. I told him that was the foolish way of doing it, that he should get Olney to file the suit, that this would put Durant behind the eight ball and force him out of business.'

'Rankin wanted him forced out of business?'

'I didn't read his mind and wouldn't tell you if I had. Durant is a fourflusher and isn't doing the game any good. I told Rankin he couldn't afford to mix his reputation up in it; that he should play it so the whole case hinged on the picture itself. So Rankin went to Olney, Olney got his attorneys, the attorneys called me and there you are.'

'And I take it you told Olney's lawyers that they had to have everything sewed up?'

'Hell, I didn't need to tell them,' Mason said. 'They're lawyers. They knew what had to be done. They got art experts to appraise the painting. They relied on me to get the affidavit that would show Durant had made the statement that it was phoney.'

'Well,' Drake said thoughtfully, 'it's a damned good vest button and it may fit on a vest. How do we start finding out?'

'First,' Mason said, 'you get your men lined up. Then I'll put in a call for Maxine at the number she left ... Take a look at that number, Della, then skip down to the office and consult your notes. You have her apartment number. See if it's her apartment and—'

'No,' Della Street said, 'it isn't her apartment, I know that. The exchange is different.'

'Okay,' Mason said, 'let's call her.'

'Now?' Drake asked.

'Now,' Mason said. 'I think having her meet me at the place where we can put shadows on her will solve the problem. I'm willing to bet that after she sees us she makes tracks to Durant. ... Paul, you get on one extension, Della get on the other and I'll talk with her while you're listening and making notes.'

'We can do better than that,' Drake said. 'I'll switch in on a recording.'

Mason grinned and said, 'You'd be too legitimate about it, Paul. You'd have a beep on it.'

Drake shook his head. 'I'm ethical, Perry, but I'm not *that* ethical.'

'All right,' Mason said, 'go ahead and record the conversation. Della, you dial the number. Paul, get your recorder running. What phone do I take, Paul?'

Drake said, 'Della dials on this phone, I listen on this one, and when she gets the party you pick up that phone, Perry. Now Della, remember that we don't want her to have an idea it's an extension phone so you say, "Just a minute, Miss Lindsay, I'll put Mr Mason on." Then you say something in a low voice into the receiver which makes it sound as if you're talking to Perry, such as "Here she is, Chief," or something of that sort.'

Della Street nodded, picked up the phone. 'All ready?' she asked.

Drake threw a switch under the desk, said to Della Street,

'Press that button for an outside line. I'm all ready.'

Drake gave one final word of caution. 'Now remember,' he said, 'don't anybody cough, don't breathe so she can hear you over the telephone. If she hears three persons breathing she'll get wise. Everybody keep absolutely quiet except the one who's doing the talking.

'Go ahead, Della.'

Della Street's nimble, trained fingers whirled the dial of the telephone. When the whirling dial had come to rest there was a moment while the phone could be heard ringing, then a thin, frightened voice said, 'Hello?'

'Miss Lindsay?' Della Street asked.

'Yes, yes,' the voice said. 'Who is this? Is this Miss Street?'

'That's right,' Della said. 'You wanted to talk with Mr Mason. He's right here, I'll put him on.'

'Oh yes, yes, please,' she said.

Della Street turned her head, spoke in a low voice and said, 'Here she is. She's on the line, Chief.'

Mason waited half a second, then said, 'Yes? Hello. Hello, Miss Lindsay, this is Perry Mason.'

'Oh, Mr Mason, I'm so glad you called. I just *had* to get in touch with you and I didn't know *what* to do.'

'What seems to be the trouble?' Mason asked.

'I'm in terrible trouble, Mr Mason. It's something private. It's something I can't confide in anyone, but I'm going to have to ... well, I'm going to have to leave and I didn't want Mr Rankin to suffer because of – well, you know – so I thought it was only fair to tell you.'

Mason said, 'Now, wait a minute, Maxine. You can't just walk out of the picture like this.'

'I'll be back,' she said. 'I'll keep in touch with you but right now something terrible has happened and I – well, I just can't be around, that's all.'

Mason caught Paul Drake's eye and winked.

'Where are you calling from, Maxine?' he asked.

'I'm not calling. You're calling me.'

'I know,' Mason said, 'but where are you? We're calling you back. This is the number you left. Is it your apartment?'

'It's— You can't try to trace me, Mr Mason. No one must know where I'm going.'

Mason said patiently, 'I'm just asking where you are *now*, Maxine, because I'd like to see if there's any possibility of seeing you personally.'

'I'm ... I'm in a telephone booth at the bus terminal. I've been waiting here for what seems interminable hours.'

'You're not at your apartment?'

'No, no, no.'

'Can I meet you at your apartment later on?'

'No, no. I'm not going back to my apartment, Mr Mason. I can't ... I can't explain. It's— No, I won't be back at my apartment.'

'All right,' Mason said. 'Now look. I want you to do one thing for me. That is, it's not for me, it's for Mr Rankin. You know Rankin has befriended you and I think you are human enough to feel at least a certain amount of gratitude towards him.'

'I do.'

'All right,' Mason said. 'Now, I've been out with Miss Street. We've been working on a case and we went to dinner and did a little dancing and I'm taking her home now.... Do you have a car?'

'Yes. I have my car near here.'

'All right,' Mason told her. 'I want you to meet us at Miss Street's apartment house. Now that will be private enough so no one will be looking for you there in case you want to keep out of sight, and you can leave you car parked with the dome light on. Miss Street and I will drive up and we can at least talk things over. You owe that much to Lattimer Rankin.'

She hesitated a moment, then said in a thin, threadlike voice, 'Yes, I guess I do.'

'You'll be there?' Mason asked.

'Where is it?'

'It's in the Crittmore Apartments on West Selig Avenue. We'll be there in about ... Well now, let's see ... It will take me about forty-five minutes to get there. Will you be there and wait for us?'

'Well ... yes, I guess so.'

'Now look, Maxine,' Mason said. 'It's terribly important. You be there, will you?'

'Yes,' she said, 'I'll be there.'

57

'You won't take a powder and run out on us?'

'No, Mr Mason. If I say I'll do a thing, I'll do it.'

'All right,' Mason told her, 'that's a good girl. Remember, Lattimer Rankin has done a lot for you and you can't go away and leave him holding the sack.'

'Oh, I . . . I do wish I – I'll be there, Mr Mason. I'll try to tell you about it.'

'Okay,' Mason said. 'Forty-five minutes.'

'Forty-five minutes,' she said, and hung up.

The three receivers in Drake's office clicked simultaneously.

'Well,' Mason said, 'what do you think of the button and the vest now, Paul?'

'Damn it, I don't know how you do it,' Drake said. 'I guess it's some kind of extrasensory perception, but you certainly called the turn.'

Della Street said, 'I've seen you pull these things often enough, Chief, so I should have known, but this time I'll admit even I was a little sceptical.'

'You were plenty sceptical,' Mason said. 'Damn it, I want to pace the floor. . . . Get on the phone, Paul, get your men going and have them down there.'

'Will my operatives need any more of a description than the one I have?' Drake asked.

Della Street said, 'She's a blonde with blue eyes, plenty of curves and—'

'Hell's bells,' Mason interrupted, 'you don't need to know what she looks like, Paul. If she's there, she'll be in a car with a dome light on, and Della Street and I will drive up and stop and talk with her. Your men can have us spotted and when she drives away they can follow her. If she isn't there, that's all there is to it.'

'You've got a point there,' Drake said. 'Okay, get the hell out of here so I can start getting men on the job. I'll have the neighbourhood of the Crittmore Apartments crawling with operatives.'

'Get them fast,' Mason said. 'Come on, Della, it will only take us twenty-five minutes to drive out there. We'll have to give Paul time enough to get his men on the job. That'll give me a few minutes to think.'

Mason held the door of Drake's office open, and Della

Street hurried ahead of him, opened the wicket gate, smiled at the night exchange operator and then held the outer door open as Perry Mason, taking a latchkey from his pocket, hurried down the corridor to his own office.

Once inside, the lawyer switched the light on and began pacing the floor.

Della Street, her eyes on her wristwatch, said, 'Are you going to let her skip out, Chief?'

'Of course I am,' Mason said. 'That's why I want Drake's men to tail her. I want to know where she goes and what she does.'

'If she's in on the fraud, could you have her arrested and—'

'And get in the same spot the jeweller gets in?' Mason said, smiling. 'No, Della. I'm just going to ride along for a while and see what it's all about.'

'It looks to me as though you know pretty well what it's all about right now.'

'Let's take it one step at a time,' Mason said. 'All I know is that Durant was putting on an act, and now that Maxine has picked up her cards and is playing them according to the old formula, I feel my suspicions were justified. I'm not going any further than that right at the moment.'

The lawyer resumed a rhythmic pacing of the floor, his thumbs hooked in his belt, his head thrust slightly forward.

Della Street, knowing that at such times he concentrated to the best advantage, sat watching him, keeping silent and from time to time glancing at her wristwatch.

'The thing all fits into a perfect formula,' Mason said at length, 'so darned perfect that it's almost a classic example.'

Since he had addressed the remark to no one in particular and obviously did not expect a reply, Della Street said nothing.

The lawyer kept on pacing.

'You can see the position I'd have been in,' he said. 'I can just see the headlines now. MILLIONAIRE SUED BY ART DEALER FOR HALF MILLION DOLLARS.... Olney's attorneys wouldn't want to take the blame. Hollister would say that I had put them up to filing the suit.... Word would get around in legal circles and everyone would be chortling at the idea of

Perry Mason, the smart criminal lawyer, being played for a sucker by a couple of bunco artists.'

'Just what do you intend to do now?' Della Street asked. 'Surely you've got to take some steps to protect yourself.'

Mason paused and said, 'The best protection is a counter-offensive, Della. I want to wait until they're ready to start their punch and then beat them to it. . . . What time is it?'

'You have another five minutes,' she said.

'I don't need it,' Mason told her, grinning. 'I think I've got it doped out now, Della. Come on, let's go.'

'Well,' Della Street said, turning out the light, 'I'm glad to see you're feeling better.'

Mason chuckled. 'In fact, Della, I think I've got it licked.'

Della Street squeezed his arm reassuringly. 'Leave it to you to come out on top,' she said.

Mason put his arm round her, patted her shoulder, and together they walked down the corridor.

'Shall I look in on Paul Drake and tell him we're on our way?' Della Street asked.

Mason hesitated a moment, then said, 'No. Probably Paul won't need the information. He's working, getting his men spotted. That's going to keep him tied up and his telephone tied up. He's expecting us to be out there.'

'And when we get there you're going to try to stall things along as much as possible?' Della Street asked.

'When I get there,' Mason said, 'we'll just play it by ear. Come on, let's go.'

Mason drove cautiously along the city streets to West Selig Avenue, then turned and slowed his speed.

'Keep an eye open, Della. Look for a car with the dome light on.'

'You don't know what kind of a car she drives?' Della Street asked.

'No. Probably one of the lighter makes and one of the older models.'

'There's a car with someone sitting in it,' Della Street said.

'A man,' Mason said. 'Don't look. That'll be one of Drake's operatives. Keep your eyes peeled for a car with the dome light on.'

'Here we are,' Della Street said. 'Up ahead, on the left.'

60

'Okay,' Mason said. 'We'll try double parking for a minute. That will give Drake's men an opportunity they can't miss.'

Mason slid his car alongside the car occupied by Maxine Lindsay.

'Hello, Maxine,' the lawyer said.

She gave them a wan smile. 'Hello.'

Mason said, 'Move over to the steering wheel so you can listen from this side, Della. Put down the window. I'll leave the door open on her car.'

Mason got out from behind the steering wheel, and Della Street promptly slid over into the position the lawyer had vacated.

The lawyer opened the door of Maxine's car, said, 'Thanks a lot for coming down here, Maxine. I was afraid you were nervous and upset and might not show up.'

She became conscious of her skirt well up above her knees as the lawyer opened the door. She made a token gesture of pulling it down an inch or two, said, 'I've been waiting here for more than ten minutes. Some man drove past and seemed ... well, he's driven past twice.'

'Someone looking for a parking place probably,' Mason said, 'or looking for a date to come out of the apartment house. Now tell me, Maxine, what's the trouble?'

She said, 'I – Mr Mason, I can't give you the details. Something terrible has happened and I have to go away.'

'All right,' Mason said, 'you're going away. Where are you going?'

'I ... I don't know – I can't tell – not even you.'

'But,' Mason said, 'you must remember you're a witness in a lawsuit.'

'I know. I understand. I gave you an affidavit. You can use that if you have to.'

'I can't use an affidavit,' Mason said. 'The law provides that a person has a right to cross-examine the witnesses called against him, and if you're going to testify against Durant, his attorneys have a right to cross-examine you.'

'That's ... that's—'

'That's what?' Mason asked.

'Nothing,' she said.

'So,' Mason told her, 'you have to be here.'

'I ... can't ... not for a while anyway.'

'All right,' Mason said, 'why can't you be here?'

'I can't tell you ... It's— No, Mr Mason, it's just too ... too terrible.

'Now please, Mr Mason, I just *can't* wait any longer. I'm in trouble and—

'Miss Street, would you do something for me?'

Della Street called across from the other car, 'What is it, Maxine?'

'My apartment,' Maxine said. 'I had to leave my canary. I'm not going to be back for – well, quite a while and I didn't have anyone I could leave the canary with. I put out feed and water to last it through tomorrow. Would you take the key to my apartment, go up tomorrow, get the bird and take it to some good pet shop that will take care of it?'

'Perhaps I could take care of it,' Della Street said, glancing significantly at Perry Mason.

'Oh, would you? Would you? That would be wonderful ! If I knew that my little bird had a home with someone who appreciated him, someone—'

'How long do you expect to be gone?' Mason asked.

'I don't know. I'll be back but I can't tell you when. I wish I knew myself. I – Mr Mason, I simply have to go. Can't you understand? I wouldn't have called you at all if I had wanted to just run out on you. I'd have gone quietly and you wouldn't have known anything about it until you started to look for me to be a witness.'

'That,' Mason admitted, 'is what puzzles me.'

'Why does it puzzle you?'

'It isn't in keeping with the rest of the picture.'

'The rest of what picture?'

'Oh, never mind,' Mason said. 'We'll work it out some way. Now, how are you going to know when I need you?'

'You just put a want ad in the paper, Mr Mason. Just say "Case coming up for trial. I need my witnesses," and sign it with just the initial M. Then I'll get in touch with you. But you'll have to arrange things so that I can be brought into court and testify and then slip right out again and— Now, let's not have any misunderstandings, Mr Mason. I'll testify to the things that are in that affidavit I signed, and that's all. I don't want to be questioned about anything else.'

'What do you mean, anything else?' Mason asked.

'Anything,' she said. 'Anything at all. . . . Now, I have to go,
Mr Mason. I simply *have* to. I can't tell you any more but I've
waited too long already.'

She handed the apartment key to Perry Mason. 'Will you
please pass this across to Miss Street?' she asked. 'Thank you
both – thank you a lot. I'm sorry things had to happen this
way but I . . . I just can't wait any longer.'

She gave Mason her hand. 'Goodbye, Mr Mason.'

The lawyer hesitated a moment, then accepting her hand,
said, 'Goodbye,' and eased himself out of the car. He closed
the car door and almost instantly Maxine started the motor.

As soon as the headlights started pulling out from the kerb,
a car half a block ahead swung out into the centre of the street.
Another car turned the corner, the driver apparently searching
for a parking place, crawling along at such a snail's pace that
he blocked traffic.

Maxine impatiently blared on the horn.

Another car coming from behind with a single masculine
driver fell in behind Maxine's car and that driver, too, impatiently blasted away on the horn.

The car that was blocking traffic moved off to one side,
and the cars that had been blocked went speeding on in a
cluster of red tail lights, all in a compact unit.

'Drake's men?' Della Street asked.

'Drake's men,' Mason said.

'Well, what do you make of it?'

Mason said, 'I don't know, Della. The lawyer in me tells me
that Durant is a phoney. On the other hand, the lawyer in me
tells me this girl is on the up-and-up and is actually in some
real trouble, that she has a horror of letting anybody down,
and that right now she intends to be present when that case is
brought up for trial.'

'In other words, your intuition is headed in two different
directions,' Della Street said, smiling.

'Reaching two opposite conclusions,' Mason said. 'A great
deal will depend on where she goes and what she does.'

'You think Drake's men will be able to follow her?'

'With a group of operatives like that,' Mason said, 'they'll follow her. The only difficulty is that she may know she's being followed.'

'What about us?' Della Street asked. 'Do we explore the apartment tonight?'

Mason shook his head. 'That key,' he said, 'could be a trap of some sort – and yet I just can't believe that girl isn't genuine. Anyhow, Miss Street, this is your apartment house and since we are here I'll take you across to your apartment and see you safely home.'

'How very nice of you,' she said, 'and what about the problem of my car, which is in the parking lot at the office building?'

'Under the circumstances,' Mason said, 'I'm quite sure the Bureau of Internal Revenue will consider that a taxicab will be a perfectly legitimate deductible expense tomorrow morning.'

'And by that time,' Della Street asked, 'you'll know where Maxine spent the night?'

'If Paul Drake's men are half as clever as they should be, we'll know from time to time *exactly* where she is. Moreover, by tomorrow morning we should know something about her past, and by tomorrow afternoon we should have a pretty good line on the terrified Maxine Lindsay.'

'Do you want the key to her apartment?' Della Street asked.

'Heavens, no. Why should I have the key to Maxine's apartment? It was given to you, Della, and in your possession it is a perfectly innocent case of keeping a canary. In my possession the situation might be a little difficult.'

'I don't get it,' Della Street said.

'Let us suppose that when Maxine gets on the witness-stand, in the event she ever does, some attorney cross-examines her and asks her casually and in parting, "Now, you read in the papers about the suit being filed by Otto Olney against Collin Durant?" And she will say, "Yes, I did," and the lawyer will say, "And on that night did you see Perry Mason, who was present at the time Olney had a Press Conference?" and she will say, "Yes, I did." And the lawyer will smirk and say, "And did you know, Miss Lindsay, that from that day on Mr Perry Mason had a key to your apartment?" Then he will smirk at the jury, bow and smile and say,

"Thank you, that's all, Miss Lindsay. I have no further questions." '

'I see,' Della Street said. 'Under the circumstances, I hang on to the key to Maxine's apartment.'

'Very definitely,' Mason said. 'You take a taxi to work in the morning, and now if you have no objection I'll move my car into the parking place vacated by Maxine Lindsay and I will escort you to your apartment.'

'That,' Della Street announced, 'is service. I welcome the suggestion. I would, however, like to know whether this is business or social.'

'It has been business to this point,' Mason said. 'The final act of escorting you to your door is social.'

'And as such?' she asked.

'I believe,' Mason observed, 'there is an almost universal custom of collecting a goodnight kiss from a date, isn't there?'

'I wouldn't know, Mr Mason,' Della said demurely.

CHAPTER SEVEN

Mason left the elevator the next morning, stopped in at the office of the Drake Detective Agency, said to the switchboard operator, 'Paul in?'

She nodded, said. 'He's busy on the phone.'

'I'll go on down,' Mason said. 'Anybody with him?'

She shook her head. 'He's alone. Just getting phone calls right and left.'

Mason smiled. 'I guess I'm responsible for that. I'll go down and listen to him gripe.'

The lawyer walked on down the narrow passageway, past the doors of the cubbyhole offices, to Paul Drake's office.

Mason opened the door.

Drake was talking on the phone. 'Okay, Bill, stay with it. Get all you can. Keep on the job. Now, is there any chance you'll need a relief up there? ... I see ... Well, it sounds a little naïve, but— Okay, if she's preoccupied, that's it.'

Drake hung up the phone, said, 'Hi, Perry,' reached for a cigarette, said, 'I've been up all night.'

'Glad to hear it,' Mason said. 'You wouldn't want to draw your money without doing something to earn it, would you?'

'Well, I'm going to draw a lot on this one,' Drake said. 'I hope your client is well heeled.'

'The client right at the moment,' Mason said, 'is Mr Perry Mason. I'm doing this on my own.'

'*You* are!' Paul Drake exclaimed, pausing with a match half-way to the cigarette.

'That's right,' Mason said. 'I'm just taking out a little insurance to see that I'm not being played for a sucker. What do you know about Maxine?'

'Maxine,' Drake said, 'is leaving a trail a mile broad. I had four operatives on the job.'

'I saw you had quite a gang,' Mason said.

'Were they obvious?'

'If you were looking for them, they were. But I had the impression Maxine was pretty much disturbed over something and wasn't paying attention to her surroundings.'

'Well, your impression was right, unless the girl is a consummate actress,' Drake said. 'She's headed for some place up north and just doesn't seem to give a hang about anything except getting there. She pulled out last night right after she talked with you, drove to an all-night drug store, parked, purchased some creams, a hairbrush, a toothbrush, comb, and a pair of pyjamas. Then she stopped at a filling station, got her car filled to the brim with gasoline and took off. She got as far as Bakersfield, went to a motel, got six hours' sleep, then was on the road again and is at the moment in Merced.'

'Stopping there?' Mason asked.

'Grabbing a bit of breakfast, getting the car filled up, and ready to be on her way again,' Drake said.

'How many men have you got on the job?' Mason asked.

'Only two at the moment,' Drake said, 'because that's all that's needed. I told the others to come on back home. I have one man keeping ahead of her, one man staying behind. They swop positions once in a while so that she doesn't feel she's wearing a tail, but frankly I don't think she's thinking about it at all.'

'What have you found out about her background?' Mason asked.

'She worked as a model in New York, she came on to Hollywood thinking she might crash the portals here, did some modelling work, started getting a little heavy, turned to a technique of photo portrait painting, and that seems to be about it.'

'Boy friends?' Mason asked.

'Haven't found any yet that she's taken any particular interest in. She seems to be pretty much in love with her work. That is, she's ambitious and keeps on plugging away at her work.

'An art dealer named Lattimer Rankin has been throwing some work her way and may have a little personal interest there. She knows a few of the models, a few of the artists, is well liked, and that's about it so far. I'm working on it. She's probably had a few affairs.'

'What about Durant?'

'Durant,' Drake said, 'is a phoney. He has some kind of a medical discharge out of the army. He dabbled around in an art appreciation course, became a self-styled art dealer, started putting on a series of lectures; talks learnedly, knows very little, is rather resourceful, likes to ride around in fancy cars which he gets second or third hand and has had a couple of them repossessed when he couldn't meet the payments. He's two months behind in the rent on his apartment and I don't think he stayed in his apartment last night. If he did, he's sleeping late this morning.

'I have a man on the job who can get in after the maids get on duty but couldn't get in last night. However, his best guess is Durant is out somewhere. His car isn't in the apartment garage. He—'

The phone rang. Drake took the cigarette out of his mouth, picked up the phone, said, 'Drake talking.'

The detective listened for a moment, said, 'Okay. That's the way I had it figured. Stay on the job until I give you instructions to the contrary.'

Drake hung up and said, 'That's the operative out at the apartment house. Durant wasn't in last night. The bed hasn't been slept in.'

'A man like that would have been married at least once,' Mason said.

'Twice we know of,' Drake said. 'Once, a young girl before he went in the army. She had a child four months after the marriage. She's working to support the child.

'After he got out of the army he married into rather a wealthy family, but he reckoned without the old man. The old man had detectives on his trail, got all the dope he needed, waited until the daughter became disillusioned and then they threw Mr Collin Durant out on his ear without a dime by way of settlement.'

'How long ago?' Mason asked.

'Four years.'

'What's he been doing since – I mean for his love life?'

'Playing the field,' Drake said. 'He has a good line of patter and he's deadly on models who pose in the nude, young female artists who want a chance to get ahead – all the general rackets.

'I haven't had a chance to check on him too much, because of the outlandish hour I started working.... My God, Perry, I've run up a bill for you. If you're footing this, it's going to give you a jolt when you get the statement, but I thought you wanted results and ... well, I sort of thought Otto Olney was the one who was back of all this and I just haven't spared expenses in order to get results.'

'Don't spare them,' Mason said. 'I want results. In fact I have to have them.

'You have a description of Durant's car?'

'Sure,' Drake said. He picked up a card, tossed it over to Mason. 'There's the make, model, licence number, colour – everything about it.'

Mason regarded the card thoughtfully.

'What about Maxine's background? Any particular reason why she should be headed where she is headed?'

'We don't know where she's headed yet,' Drake said. 'It could be Sacramento, it could be Eugene, it could be Portland, it could be Seattle, it could be Canada. Give her time. One thing's certain. She's headed on a long trip, she's short of cash, and she's trying to get where she's going in a hurry.'

'How do you know she's short of cash?'

68

'Haggling over the motel room, for one thing. It took her half an hour in Bakersfield to find a place where the rate suited her. She's drinking coffee and not eating much. She started out with premium gasoline; then she started mixing premium and standard, now she's running on standard grade gasoline.'

'No credit card?' Mason asked.

'No credit card. She's paying cash.'

'Okay,' Mason said, 'stay with her, Paul. I'll be seeing you.'

Mason left the detective, walked on down the corridor, opened the door of the private office, and said to Della, 'Well, how did it go?'

'Wonderful,' Della Street said.

'Good night's sleep?''

'Fine.'

'And you took a cab to work?'

She smiled and said, 'No, Chief, I didn't. I knew that this was on you, that you weren't going to bill Olney, so I took one bus, transferred, took another bus and got here right on the nose.'

Mason frowned. 'You should have taken a cab.'

'I saved you four dollars and ninety cents,' she said, 'not including a tip.'

Mason was thoughtful a moment, then said, 'It's that spirit of loyalty that makes me feel . . .'

'Yes?' Della prompted.

'Sort of humble,' Mason said. 'I hope I can deserve it.'

'What do you hear from Drake?' she asked abruptly. 'I told him I thought you'd stop in on your way here.'

'I stopped in,' Mason said. 'Durant has holed up somewhere and disappeared.'

'What about Maxine?'

'Maxine is making tracks north. She's just about running out of cash.'

The phone rang.

Della Street picked it up, said, 'It's Paul, Perry.'

Mason picked up the telephone on his desk and said, 'What is it, Paul?'

'Another line on your friend, Maxine Lindsay.'

'What about her?'

'She wired Mrs Phoebe Stigler at Eugene, Oregon, to wire

twenty-five dollars to her care of Western Union, Redding, and waive identification.'

'How do you know?'

'She wired from Merced,' Drake said. 'My man got on the job, insisted the girl at the counter had lost the telegram he'd handed her and she started looking through the file. My man became thoroughly disliked but got a look at the wire Maxine had sent.'

'Okay, Paul,' Mason said. 'Check on Phoebe Stigler at Eugene. Find out all about her.'

The telephone rang. Della Street picked up the instrument and said, 'Yes, Gertie? What is it? ... Just a minute.'

She turned to Perry Mason and said, 'Mr Hollister of Warton, Warton, Cosgrove, and Hollister, is calling.'

Mason's eyes narrowed. 'All right,' he said. 'I'll take it.'

He picked up the telephone, said, 'Good morning, Mr Hollister. How's everything this morning?'

'Perhaps not so good,' Hollister said.

'In what respect?' Mason asked.

'This witness, Maxine Lindsay.'

'What about her?'

'I have been analysing the situation,' Hollister said, 'and our whole case hinges upon her, and upon the availability of her testimony.'

'Well?' Mason asked.

'At the start I had of course thought that the situation hinged upon the question of whether the painting which Rankin had sold our client, Otto Olney, was a genuine Phellipe Feteet.

'I had felt that since Rankin's veracity and integrity as a dealer had been put into question, the main issue in the case would depend upon establishing the authenticity of the painting which Rankin had sold our client.'

'Exactly,' Mason said.

'However, there seems to be absolutely no question about the authenticity of the painting. It would seem that the way the situation shapes up at present, the only issue of fact is whether Durant made the statement that the painting was spurious. Now, it has occurred to us this morning that this hinges entirely upon the testimony of one witness.

'I may point out to you, Mr Mason, that we have an office conference every morning at eight-thirty, discussing the problems which we have in connection with our litigation, and Mr Warton, our senior partner, pointed out that the entire litigation at this point seems to depend upon establishing the fact that Durant made this remark, and that in turn is dependent upon the testimony of only one witness.'

'Well, one witness can establish a point all right,' Mason said.

'You have no question but what that witness is acting in good faith?'

'Why should I?' Mason asked.

'Suppose,' Hollister said, 'that – well, suppose this witness should marry Collin Durant before the case came to trial. Then she would be unable to testify against her husband and my client would find himself in a very precarious position.'

'Did you have any information on which to base that?' Mason asked.

'No information – one of the partners raised the point.'

Mason said, 'I don't have any partners, Hollister, and therefore I don't have any office conferences with people who think up things to worry about.'

'I thought I'd let you know our thinking in the matter,' Hollister said stiffly.

'Okay,' Mason said, 'why not cut the Gordian knot right now? Why not serve notice on Durant that you're going to take his deposition? Why not ask him the question right out in the open, did he or did he not make a statement to Maxine Lindsay that the Phellipe Feteet that was hanging in the saloon of Otto Olney's yacht was a fake?'

'I've thought of that,' Hollister said.

'Well, what's wrong with it?'

'I guess there's nothing wrong with it. I ... I'll – I think I'll discuss that with my partners.'

'Do that,' Mason said. 'If the fellow says he never made any such statement, then you know what his defence is. If he says he made it and the picture is spurious, then you know what you're up against. In any event, let's find out what the score is. ... What makes you think she's going to marry Durant?'

'Well, at our partnership meeting we just started thinking

71

about what could happen, what the possibilities were. If something should happen that ... Well, that we had got our client out on a limb, we wouldn't like that, Mr Mason.'

'I wouldn't like it either,' Mason said.

'Well, I'm glad to have had this opportunity to talk with you,' Hollister said. 'The more I think of it, the more I feel that we should find out where we stand and I think taking Durant's deposition is perhaps the best course immediately available. I will prepare the necessary papers and we'll proceed at once.'

'Do that,' Mason said.

He hung up the phone, turned to Della Street, said, 'Here we are standing on a rug with somebody ready to jerk it out from under us.'

'So what do we do?' Della Street asked.

Mason grinned and said, 'Spike the rug down so that when the guy jerks, he loses a set of fingernails.'

'What do we do next?' Della Street asked.

'Now,' Mason said, 'we gently ease ourselves out of the office without telling anyone where we're going, and we go to the apartment of Maxine Lindsay and see just what we can find.'

'You mean we take the canary?'

'We take the canary,' Mason said, 'and while we're there we go through the place with a fine-toothed comb. We look for any sort of clue we can get.'

'And then what?'

'Then,' Mason said, 'we ask Mr Hollister of Warton, Warton, Cosgrove, and Hollister if he would like to have associate counsel in the case.'

'The associate counsel being who?'

'Being me,' Mason said. 'It's about time someone with guts got into the thing. We take the deposition of Collin Durant. We ask him a series of the most embarrassing questions imaginable. We ask him whether he has ever been sued before for proclaiming a painting spurious. We ask him whether he did or did not state that the Otto Olney Feteet was spurious. We ask him how long he has known Maxine Lindsay. We ask him if he has ever been married. We ask him the names of his wives. We ask him the places where he got divorces.'

'Is all that pertinent?'

'Sure, it's pertinent,' Mason said. 'If the guy thinks he's going to sneak up to Oregon and marry Maxine and then come back here and smile at us, we're going to try to prevent it. We're going to see if all his previous marriages have been dissolved or whether one may still be in force. If we can find a valid outstanding marriage, we're going to arrest the guy for bigamy the minute he marries Maxine, and then we're going to force Maxine to testify on the ground that she isn't the legal wife of Collin Durant. It seems that the guy is the marrying kind, and if this lawsuit racket is a habit with him, he's married other witnesses to keep them from testifying.'

'What makes you think they're having a rendezvous to get married in Oregon?' Della Street asked.

'Well, we'll look at it this way. Where is Collin Durant? He hasn't been home, his car is missing, and Maxine was in a hurry. She had to leave last night. She evidently had a meeting place that had been definitely pinpointed somewhere.'

'It begins to add up,' Della Street admitted.

'Come on,' Mason said, 'let's go.'

'Are you going to tell Paul where we're going?'

'We won't tell anyone,' Mason said.

After they were in Mason's car, Della said, 'She gave me a key. That makes anything we do legal, doesn't it?'

'She gave you a key in order to get the canary,' Mason said, 'but something seems to tell me you won't be able to find the feed for the canary and you'll have to look around some to find out where she kept it.'

'In the kitchen?' Della Street asked.

'Well, of course you can't tell with a girl like Maxine,' Mason said. 'She might have kept it in the bedroom or in one of the closets. Or again, it might have been in a suitcase somewhere, or down in the bottom of a bureau drawer. A package of birdseed could be kept almost anywhere – and then of course there's cuttlebone. I think you have to use cuttlebone to keep a canary healthy and – oh, I can think of lots of things that might be around there in various places.'

'So we're going to look in various places.'

'Don't make any mistake, Della, we're going to look in *all* the places.'

They drove in silence, Della Street apparently speculating on the various possibilities.

Mason said, 'We don't need to go blind very much longer, Della. The trail is pretty well blazed. The fact that Warton, Warton, Cosgrove, and Hollister are beginning to worry is something to think about. If this is a racket, it's about time some lawyer shows up stating he represents Durant and wants to start talking settlement.'

'And you think Olney will settle?'

Mason said, 'His attorneys are corporation attorneys. They aren't accustomed to rough-and-tumble fighting. They begin to realize now what a horrible mess their client *could* be in and naturally they don't want to have it get around the courthouse that they got Olney out on a limb, any more than I want to have it get around that *I* got a client out on a limb. The only difference is that when the going gets tough I'll fight regardless of whether the situation is disagreeable. I don't think those other lawyers will.'

Della Street said, 'This is her apartment house. We should be able to find a parking place at this hour of the morning—Here's one right here.'

Mason said, 'That's rather a long walk. I think we can find one closer.'

He suddenly braked the car to a stop.

'What's the matter?' Della asked.

'That car,' Mason said, pointing to a large pretentious automobile parked at the kerb.

'What about it?'

'It's the same general description as Collin Durant's. I got the description from Paul Drake just a short time ago – and I think it's the same licence number. Skip out and take a look at the registration on the steering post, will you, Della?'

Della whipped open the door of the car, jumped to the ground, took a quick look at the registration then hurried back to the car and said, 'That's right, it's Collin Max Durant's automobile.'

'The plot thickens all to hell,' Mason said. 'Now, what do you suppose Durant is doing here?'

'Trying to see Maxine?' Della Street asked.

'In that event,' Mason said, 'he has been here for a long

74

time, or else the guy likes to walk. When he parked his car, there weren't many parking places available near the apartment house, which means either that the people hadn't gone to work early in the morning or that he came in at night after people had come home from the offices and had taken up most of the readily available parking spaces.'

'Well, since we know she wasn't in her apartment all last night,' Della Street said, 'that would seem to indicate he had come this morning and—'

'Or has been waiting for her all night,' Mason said, 'in which event he probably found some means of letting himself into her apartment.'

'Perhaps he has a key.'

'Could be,' Mason said. 'Those things *have* happened.'

The lawyer eased his car into motion and drove up to one of the vacant parking places near the main entrance to the apartment house.

'What's her number, Della?' he asked.

'Three-thirty-eight-B.'

'Well,' Mason said, 'we'll go up and see what gives.'

'If he's waiting in the apartment, what do we do?' she asked.

'Play it by ear,' Mason said. 'But I think we get tough. If it's a fight he wants, we can let him know it's going to go the limit.'

They went up in the elevator, oriented themselves on numbers, walked to Apartment 338-B, and Della Street silently handed Mason the key.

Mason carefully inserted the key in the lock so as not to make the slightest noise, pressed gently against the key. Nothing happened. 'The wrong key?' Della asked.

Mason tried the knob. 'No, the door seems to have been left unlocked.' He twisted the knob, pushed open the door.

The apartment was empty and in perfect order.

Mason stood in the doorway, looking the place over. Della Street, standing directly behind him, placed one of her hands on his arm.

'No one's here,' she said.

'That's either a kitchenette out there or a bedroom,' Mason said. 'Probably a kitchenette.'

The lawyer gently closed the door of the apartment, crossed over to the swinging door, pushed it open to disclose a tidy kitchenette with a pocket-sized refrigerator.

'There must be a wall bed,' Mason said. 'Apparently that's all there is to the place, except there's a bath.'

Mason walked over, opened the door to the bathroom, then recoiled.

Della Street stifled a scream.

The body of a man was lying face down, the legs sprawled across the tiles, the upper part of the body lying in the shower stall.

Mason bent over the body.

'Is it . . .?' Della Street's voice failed.

Mason said, 'It's Collin M. Durant, our obnoxious friend of last night, and he's dead as a mackerel. Evidently these are bullet holes in the back.'

Mason bent over to touch the still form.

'How long has he been dead?' she asked.

'That,' Mason said, 'is going to be *the* big question. Notice that all the lights are on, Della.'

'Then he must have come up here after he left us last night,' Della Street said. 'The lights are on. Maxine would normally have turned them off – and Durant's bed wasn't slept in last night.'

'And,' Mason said, 'was he up here *before* Maxine left her apartment or not? Can Maxine prove that she was waiting at a pay station telephone booth? We've got to get Homicide on the job right away, Della. Minutes are precious. They've got to determine the time of death and let's not throw any obstacle in the way of an accurate determination— Hello, what's this?'

'What?' Della Street asked.

Mason turned back the coat slightly. 'Look at that inside pocket,' he said, 'filled with hundred-dollar bills. And this is the boy who lost a couple of cars because he couldn't keep up the payments, the man who was two months behind in the rent on his apartment, the fourflushing playboy who didn't have any ready cash.'

'How much is in there?' Della Street asked.

'Heaven knows,' Mason said, 'and I don't want to take the

responsibility of counting it. We're not supposed to touch anything.'

The lawyer straightened.

'How long does it take *rigor mortis* to develop?' Della Street asked.

'It's a variable,' Mason said. 'It depends on temperature, on the activity of the body just prior to death, on the degree of excitement. It usually takes eight to twelve hours, but it can last for eighteen hours after it develops. Notice that *rigor* has fully developed in this body and hasn't as yet begun to leave.'

Della Street said, 'Good heavens! This changes the complexion of the entire case, doesn't it?'

'It not only changes the complexion,' Mason said slowly and thoughtfully, 'it changes the case. Come on, Della, we've got to telephone Homicide and let our friend, Lieutenant Tragg, interrogate us as to how it happened we discovered another body.'

They started for the door. Abruptly Mason said, 'Della, I'm going to have to put you out on the firing line.'

'What do you mean?'

'*You're* going to have to telephone Homicide and tell them the story.'

'What story do I tell them?'

'Tell them that Maxine Lindsay was a witness in a case, that while I was not an attorney of record I was interested in the case, that she told you last night she was leaving and gave you the key to her apartment and asked you to see about the canary.'

'Heavens, yes, the canary,' Della Street said. 'I almost forgot about it. Where is it?'

'And *that's* a good question,' Mason said, looking around the place. 'There isn't any sign of a cage, no sign of a bird – no sign that there ever was a bird – nothing to indicate that she ever owned a canary.'

Della Street exchanged glances with the lawyer. 'And what would *that* mean?' she asked.

'That might mean lots of things,' Mason said. 'Della, be very, very careful. Tell the police the exact truth about the time that we met Maxine. Don't tell them about the time she telephoned us, about the number she gave us, the place where she said she was.'

Della Street said, 'Gosh, Chief, I just made a note of that number long enough to call her and then tossed it in the wastebasket because she said it wasn't her apartment but was a phone booth.'

Mason's eyes were thoughtful. 'Tell them she gave you the key to her apartment,' he said. 'Tell them that you don't feel that you can tell anyone what reason she gave until you have an okay from me. She gave you the key to her apartment and that's all – that's it, period. You took the key and came up here with me. You can't tell them anything about the case until you have my permission. You must, however, tell them everything connected with the discovery of the body, all about the time and how we happened to be here, and that we found the door unlocked.'

'Do I tell them you were here with me?'

'Sure.'

'And where do I tell them that you are? They'll want to know.'

'Tell them I couldn't be detained at the moment, I had to go out on business. They'll be furious but with me, not with you.'

'Aren't you supposed to report a body just as soon as you find it? Aren't you supposed to hold yourself available and—'

'I'm reporting it,' Mason said. 'That is, you are, and you're my employee. What I do through my agents I do myself. On the other hand, I can't afford to stick around for a lot of police questioning right at the moment. I'm going to have to go places.'

'Where?' Della Street asked.

Suddenly before Mason could answer she said, 'Oh, I know. You're taking a plane north.'

'Exactly,' Mason said, 'and you're not to tell anyone where I'm going and we aren't going to let the police know anything about Paul Drake being on the job and putting a lot of shadows on Maxine. We'll tell them that later.'

'Can you get there in time?' Della Street asked.

'I think so,' Mason said. 'I'll get a plane to San Francisco and then charter a plane if I have to. I may be able to get a through plane to Sacramento and then pick up a Pacific Airlines planes or charter one. Anyway, I'll get there, Della.'

'And I'm to tell no one where you are.'

'That's right,' Mason said. 'You don't know.'

'And I telephone the police now?'

'Right now,' Mason said. 'Ask for Lieutenant Tragg at Homicide – and you'd better lock up here and use the phone in the lobby. There may be fingerprints on that telephone the police would like to save.'

Mason gently turned the knob and held the door open for Della Street.

'Take the elevator,' he said. 'I can beat it going down the stairs. You'll have to take a cab back to the office.'

The lawyer hurried to the stairway, took the stairs two at a time.

CHAPTER EIGHT

It was three-thirty in the afternoon when the taxicab Perry Mason had taken at the Redding Airport deposited him at the Western Union Telegraph office.

Mason, with his most disarming smile, said, 'My name is Stigler. I had twenty-five dollars wired to my wife's sister, Maxine Lindsay, from Eugene with identification waived. I'm wondering if she's picked up the money yet.'

The clerk hesitated a moment, then consulted files and said, 'No, Mr Stigler, she hasn't.'

'Thank you,' Mason said. 'I hoped I could get here ahead of her. She may need more than that. Thanks a lot. I'll wait outside. She should be here any minute.'

Mason went out to the street, found a phone booth at a service station where he could keep an eye on the telegraph office and put through a call to Paul Drake.

'Hello, Paul,' Mason said. 'I'm up in Redding. She hasn't picked up the wire yet. Do you know where she is?'

'She should be there almost any minute,' Drake said. 'My

man reported from Chico. She stopped there and had something to eat, had her tyres checked, had gas put in the car. She didn't have the tank filled. She only had enough gas put in to get her through to Redding. She's evidently right down to her last penny but she should be showing up.'

'Thanks,' Mason said. 'I'll wait for her here.'

'What about my operatives?' Drake asked. 'Do you want them to keep on after you take over?'

'I'll have to let you know on that,' Mason said, 'but have them stay on the job unless I give you instructions to call them off. And of course they aren't supposed to give me a tumble in case they recognize me.'

'Hell's bells,' Drake said disgustedly, 'these are professionals. Don't worry. You may not even be able to spot them.'

Mason hung up the telephone, walked out to stand at the kerb. He had been there about twenty minutes when Maxine Lindsay, her eyes slightly bloodshot, her face grey with weariness, drove up and slowed to a crawl as she looked for a parking place.

Eventually she settled on the service station from which Mason had been telephoning. She drove the car in and said, 'Can I leave my car here while I go to the telegraph office long enough to get some money? Then I'm going to want my tank filled up.'

'I'll fill it now, ma'am, and you can pay when you get back,' the attendant said.

'No, I . . . I prefer it this way. I'm expecting some money at the telegraph office but if I don't get it I might not be able to pay.'

The attendant looked at her sympathetically and said, 'I'll park it right over here, ma'am. I'm sure you'll have the money waiting for you.'

'Oh, I hope so,' Maxine told him, giving him a wan smile, and then leaving the car started walking wearily down the sidewalk.

She was so thoroughly tired that she hardly noticed when Mason fell into step beside her.

At length sensing the presence of someone keeping pace with her she glanced up with annoyance. 'I beg your pardon, if you—'

She gasped, faltered, came to a dead stop.

'I'm sorry I had to do it this way, Maxine,' Mason said, 'but we have to talk.'

'I – You— How in the world did you get here?'

'By making good connections at Sacramento with a Pacific Airlines plane,' Mason said. 'Are you tired, Maxine?'

'I'm bushed.'

'Hungry?'

'I had something to eat in Chico. I couldn't go any longer. I'd been living on coffee. It took my last dime.'

'All right,' Mason said, 'there's twenty-five dollars waiting for you at the telegraph office. Shall we go and get that?'

'How . . . how in the world do you know all these things?'

'It's my business,' Mason said. 'Twenty-five dollars sent to you by Phoebe Stigler from Eugene, Oregon.'

'All right,' Maxine said, 'if you know that much I presume you know the rest of it.'

Mason smiled enigmatically. 'Let's go get the money, Maxine, and then we'll sit down over a cup of coffee and talk.'

'I haven't got time,' she said. 'I've got to get on. I've just got to keep slogging along that damned road and I'm *so* tired.'

'Come on,' Mason said, 'let's get the money and then we'll talk it over. Perhaps you won't have to keep on hurrying.'

The lawyer walked into the telegraph office, smiled and nodded at the clerk, pushed Maxine forward.

'Do you have a wire for me, Maxine Lindsay?' she asked.

'Yes, we do, Miss Lindsay. Will you sign here, please? You were expecting some money?'

'That's right.'

'How much?'

'Twenty-five dollars.'

'Who from?'

'Phoebe Stigler of Eugene, Oregon.'

'Just sign here, please.'

Maxine signed her name, the clerk handed her two tens and a five and exchanged smiles with Mason.

Mason placed his hand on Maxine's elbow and said, 'Come on, we'll go get that car filled up and then get a cup of coffee.'

They walked back to the filling station where Maxine left

instructions about the car, then went across to a restaurant. Maxine slumped into a seat in a booth and rested her chin on her hand.

'You've had quite a drive,' Mason said. 'You shouldn't be going on until you've had some sleep.'

'I've got to get there. I've simply got to get there.'

Mason told the waitress, 'Fill up two coffee cups and bring a pitcher with coffee in it.

'Cream, sugar?' he asked Maxine.

She shook her head and said, 'No more. It puts on too many inches.'

The waitress looked at Mason inquiringly.

'Just black for me,' Mason said.

The waitress left and in a short time returned with two cups of coffee, then brought two small metal pots.

'We use these for hot water, mostly,' she said, 'but I've filled them up with coffee.'

'That's fine,' Mason told her and handed her a five-dollar bill. 'Please take care of the check for us,' he said, 'and put the rest in your pocket. We don't want to be disturbed.'

The face of the waitress lit up. She said, 'Oh, thank you. Thank you very much. Is there anything else I can do?'

'Not a thing.'

'If there's anything you want, just hold up your hand. I'll be watching.'

Maxine put a spoon in the coffee, stirred it, raised the spoon to her lips, sipped the coffee tentatively to determine the temperature, then again settled back into a dejected attitude.

'Now, you wanted us to look after the canary,' Mason said.

She looked up and barely nodded.

'But,' Mason said, 'there wasn't any canary.'

She had started to raise the coffee cup to her lips, looking at Mason with tired eyes. Suddenly she became alert, holding the coffee cup arrested half-way to her lips.

'There wasn't *what*?'

'There wasn't any canary,' Mason said.

'What are you talking about? Of course there's a canary! Dickey was there in his cage. . . . He's the one I was worrying about.'

'There wasn't any canary,' Mason said.

'But, Mr Mason . . . I don't understand. . . . There had to be. Dickey was there. Dickey, the canary.'

'No canary,' Mason said, 'but there was something else.'

'What do you mean, something else?'

'A corpse,' Mason said, 'in your shower.'

The coffee cup wobbled as she started to put it back on the saucer.

'The corpse of Collin Durant, sprawled in your shower, shot in the back, very, very dead. He . . .'

The coffee cup dropped from her nerveless fingers. Hot coffee spilled over the table. Not until some of it trickled to her lap and the hot liquid had burned through her dress did Maxine scream.

Mason held up his hand.

The attentive waitress was instantly on the job.

'We've had an accident,' Mason said.

The waitress gave Mason a shrewd, searching look. Then, with her face a mask, said, 'I'll get a towel. Would you like to move over to another booth?'

Maxine moved out into the aisle, shook her skirt, took a napkin and sponged at the coffee stain. Her face seemed as white as the plaster on the wall.

'Right in here and sit down,' Mason said.

The waitress appeared with a towel, mopped up the spilled coffee, hurried away to get another cup of coffee and brought it back to them in the next booth.

Mason said, 'Now, get hold of yourself. Are you trying to tell me that you didn't know Durant's body was in your apartment when you gave Della Street the key and told her to go up?'

'Honest, Mr Mason, I didn't. . . . You aren't lying to me, are you?'

'*I'm* telling *you* the truth.'

'That,' she said, after a moment, 'changes things a lot.'

'I thought it would,' Mason said. 'Perhaps you'd like to tell me how.'

'You're not – you're not trying to trap me, are you, Mr Mason?'

'What do you mean?'

'Collin Durant is— He's really dead?'

'He's dead,' Mason said. 'He was evidently shot in the back, perhaps two or three times. His body fell forward in your bathroom. I wouldn't want to make anything more than a guess right now but as a guess I'd say that he was searching the apartment when he was killed, that he stepped into the bathroom, parted the shower curtains, and that, as he did so, someone put a small-calibre revolver right up against the back of his coat and pulled the trigger two or three times. Now, does that mean anything to you?'

She said, 'I didn't do it, if that's what you want to know.'

'Suppose,' Mason said, 'you tell me a little bit about Durant.'

'Durant was a . . . a devil.'

'Go on,' Mason said.

She said, 'Durant had the most horrible pair of ears in the world. He heard everything and he forgot nothing. He would encourage people to talk, getting them to tell about their own affairs, about their own background. He'd be the most attentive, sympathetic listener in the world, and he'd be remembering everything he heard. Sometimes I think he must have gone home and put everything on a tape-recorder or something and kept notebooks.

'He'd pick up every piece of gossip, every little thing from lots of different people and then he'd start correlating them, putting them all together, fitting them into a pattern until gradually he knew more about you than you could possibly realize.'

'Blackmail?' Mason asked.

'It wasn't exactly blackmail,' she said. 'It was trying to build himself up, trying to get what he wanted, trying to get influence. I don't think he used it for money but— Still, I don't know.'

'How long had you known him?'

'Nearly three years.'

'And what was his hold on you?'

She looked up at Mason, then lowered her eyes, started to say something, checked herself.

'Go on,' Mason said. 'I'm going to find out anyway. You may as well tell me.'

She said after a moment, 'He knew certain things about me.'

'I gathered as much,' Mason said dryly and waited for her to go on.

She didn't go on, but sipped her coffee with weary resignation.

'All right,' Mason said, 'let's begin on another angle. Who's Phoebe Stigler?'

'My sister.'

'Married?'

'Oh, yes.'

'Happily?'

'Very happy.'

'What's her husband's name?'

'Homer Hardin Stigler. He's a big real estate operator and financier in Eugene.'

'What,' Mason asked, 'was Durant's hold on you?'

'I can't tell you. I won't tell you.'

'Why?' Mason asked.

'Because it . . . it's something I wouldn't tell anyone.'

'Come, come,' Mason said, 'the world has moved a long way since the time when some purple chapter in a girl's history would—'

She said, 'Oh, don't be *silly*! It isn't anything of *that* sort. After all, Mr Mason, I've been around. I've made a living being an artists' model. I'm not a prude and I'm not dumb.'

Mason watching her shrewdly tried a shot in the dark. 'I know,' he said sympathetically, 'it's not that it involves you, but it does involve your sister.'

She stiffened as though she had been shocked with an electric current. 'What are you saying? . . . What do you know?'

'I know a great deal,' Mason said, 'and I intend to find out more – if I have to.'

'How could you possibly find those things out?'

'The way I find out everything,' Mason said. 'It costs money but I get the information. How did I know you were here? How did I know you had wired your sister to send you twenty-five dollars here and waive identification? How did I know where you were? How did I know that you had a hard time finding a motel you felt you could afford last night in Bakersfield?'

'How *do* you know these things?' she asked.

'I make it my business to find out,' Mason told her. 'I have to do it. If you want to tell me about your sister, I'll try and co-operate as far as I can. If you don't tell me, I'll find out anyway and then I won't be under any obligations.'

'You mustn't – you mustn't ask questions, particularly around Eugene. That would be . . .'

She broke off as though the mere contemplation of what might happen filled her with panic.

'Then,' Mason said, 'you'd better tell me of your own accord so I'll know what to do and what not to do.'

Maxine hesitated for a moment, then refilled the coffee cup from the container, closed her eyes wearily, said, 'I just don't have the strength to struggle, Mr Mason. I— No, I'm not going to tell you. I can't, but Durant had a hold on me.'

'And,' Mason said, 'he had a good racket. He'd brand a painting as a forgery, have you pass the word that he'd de-clared it a forgery. Then when a lawsuit was filed, you'd skip out and not be available. How many times has he worked this?'

'He's never worked it. I didn't know he ever did anything of the sort,' she said.

'The painting Lattimer Rankin sold that was supposed to have been forged?'

She said, 'I just don't understand that. There's something weird about that.'

'Go on,' Mason said. 'Tell me what happened.'

'Well,' she said, 'we were at this party and Durant told me the painting was a forgery. I got mad because I knew that Rankin had sold that painting and I knew he wouldn't be fooled on a matter of that sort and I didn't like the idea of Collin Durant talking that way and I told him so. And he dared me to go and tell Rankin what he had said, then he told me I must tell him.'

'So then what?'

'I thought it over for a while and then went to Mr Rankin. I didn't really intend to tell him what Collin had said, but I did ask him if there could be any possible doubt about the authen-ticity of that painting, and Rankin said heavens no and wanted to know why I was asking. . . . Finally he got the whole story out of me and was furious.

86

'So then I became frightened. I simply couldn't have Collin angry with me. So I told him about my conversation with Rankin.'

'Was he angry?' Mason asked.

'No, he was pleased. He said I'd done exactly what he wanted. He told me that I was to stay with it, that if Rankin went to a lawyer and they asked me to make an affidavit that I was to tell exactly what had happened and swear to it.

'He said he wanted Rankin to see a lawyer. He was tremendously pleased – that is, at first.'

'Go ahead,' Mason said.

'Well, of course my talk with Rankin started things. The next thing I knew you were sending for me and asking me questions and wanting me to sign an affidavit.'

'And then what happened?'

She said, 'Your secretary, Della Street, may not remember it but while she was preparing the affidavit I said I wanted to call a friend of mine. The person I called was Collin Durant. I told him that I found myself in your office and that your secretary was preparing an affidavit for me to sign.'

'And what did he say?'

'He laughed and told me that was exactly what he wanted and to go ahead and sign it. He said he wanted me to be a witness.'

'Then what?'

'Then the suit was filed and there was that newspaper publicity and then Durant came to me and told me I had to get out of the country.'

'Now, that was last night?' Mason asked.

'Yes. Things have been happening so fast it seems like a week ago. Yes, it was last night.'

'Now then,' Mason said, 'this is important. It's very important. What time was it that he came to you?'

'It was about six o'clock.'

Mason said, 'Then that would have been an hour or an hour and a half before he came to me.'

'He saw *you* yesterday?'

'That's right. He came to me in a restaurant and told me that you were a publicity seeker, that you were trying to stir up trouble in order to further your own interests, and that no little trollop, as he expressed it, was going to bounce her curves off his reputation just in order to bask in the limelight.'

'And that was when?'

'That was no later than seven-thirty,' Mason said.

'But I can't understand it,' she said. 'He *wanted* me to tell Rankin.'

Mason said, 'Let's get this straight. He came to you yesterday and told you you had to leave the country, didn't he?'

'He told me that I had to disappear, yes. That I had to get out of town so that no one could find me. He said that I mustn't be available so that my deposition could be taken and that I mustn't be a witness, and that I would have to go where you couldn't find me.'

'And you started right away?'

'No, no. He was coming back.'

'What was he coming back for?'

'To give me money.'

'To give *you* money?'

'That's right.'

'As a bribe?'

'No, no. As travelling expenses. I was to get started and I was to go down to Mexico and just disappear.'

'And he was going to give you your travelling expenses?'

'That's right.'

'When?'

'Well, he came there about six o'clock and told me that he'd be back within an hour with money if he could get it. If he wasn't back in an hour with the money, I was to leave the apartment, go to the bus terminal and wait for him there. He said he'd be there if he missed me at the apartment.'

'He didn't come back to the apartment?'

'He never came.'

'So what did you do?'

'I waited for a good hour and then left the place and went to the bus terminal, just as he had told me to. I was in a panic. I didn't really have money enough to travel, but Collin had told me to get out – and he meant it.'

'He told you he wanted you to be where I couldn't find you?'

'Yes. He said you'd try to take my deposition and he couldn't have that happen.'

'Yet in spite of that you got in touch with me?'

'Yes.'

'I'm afraid I don't understand.'

'Don't you see? I couldn't call you from my apartment or from anyplace where he'd know I was calling. But you'd been so nice ... I hated to let you down. So I went to the bus terminal. I was to meet him there if he didn't get to the apartment in an hour. He said to wait there at the terminal until eight o'clock.'

'And you decided to risk a call to me?'

'Yes. I wanted to let you know I was leaving – I felt you were entitled to that much. I remembered what you'd told me about getting in touch with the Drake Detective Agency after office hours and I called them and told them I simply had to get in touch with you.

'I felt you'd protect my confidence and Durant would never know I called you.... Well, then it got past eight o'clock and he didn't show up at the terminal as he had promised. I was desperate. I left the number there – and then you called. I just wanted to tell you I was leaving – but you wanted to see me – and by that time I'd made up my mind Durant wasn't going to meet me or give me any money and that I'd have to get out on my own.... So I decided to meet you and explain as much as I dared, and then drive up to my sister's place. I knew Durant could locate me there if he really wanted ... and give me the money to go to Mexico.'

Mason said, 'Maxine, I'm not your attorney, but I do feel that I should tell you one thing in fairness to you.'

'What?'

'The police are going to look at things in an entirely different manner than you do.'

'Oh, I suppose so,' she said wearily.

'Now, wait a minute,' Mason said, 'pay attention. The police are going to think that Durant had some hold on you, that he was trying to get you to do something that you didn't want to do.'

'Well, they're right. I told you that, Mr Mason. I'd admit it.'

'And,' Mason went on, 'that Durant told you he was coming back to your place with money – not at six-thirty, not at seven-thirty, but at about eight o'clock. That he came up there at eight o'clock. That you had an argument. That he was telling you what you had to do and you didn't want to do it. That he was a shrewd chiseller who was holding something over you and he had an idea that perhaps you had a detective concealed in the apartment somewhere so he decided to reassure himself as to that before he committed himself by making any statements.

'He looked in the kitchenette, then he looked in the bathroom, jerked the curtains of the shower aside to see if you had someone planted there, and that as he stood there with his back to you, you whipped a gun out of your purse and shot him in the back. Then you dashed out, tried to communicate with me, made up all this story about what he was doing, and all this song and dance about the canary and gave Della Street the key to your apartment with the idea that she was to go and get the canary; that you did all this simply so you could get out of the state and have a headstart; and that when Della Street went to the apartment and discovered Durant's body and noticed the police, you'd have a story to tell and an alibi of sorts.'

'Good heavens, Mr Mason, I didn't kill him. I—'

'I'm telling you what the police are going to think,' Mason said, 'and the assumption on which they're going to work.'

'They could never prove anything like that,' she said, 'because it isn't so, not any of it. I didn't kill him.'

'Can you prove you didn't?' Mason asked.

She looked at him with dawning apprehension on her face.

'After all,' Mason said, 'he was killed in your apartment and while they haven't found the murder weapon yet, there's always a chance that . . .'

The lawyer broke off at the look on her face.

'I see I'm beginning to register now,' he said.

'The gun that killed him. What kind of a gun was it?'

'Apparently a small-calibre revolver,' Mason said.

'I . . . I—'

'Go on,' Mason told her.

'I had such a gun in the apartment. I kept it right in the dresser drawer for protection.'

Mason's smile was sceptical.

'You *must* believe me, Mr Mason, you simply *must*!'

'I'd like to,' Mason said. 'You make a good impression. But after all, Maxine, this is your first attempt at concocting a story. Remember, I've heard hundreds of them.'

'But this isn't a story that I'm concocting. It's the truth.'

Mason said, 'I know, Maxine. You go ahead and handle it the way you want to. I just felt that it was my duty to point out to you that the police were going to build a case against you.'

'But what can I do?'

'I don't know,' Mason told her, 'and remember this, Maxine. I am not your lawyer. I would suggest that you go from here to the best lawyer in Redding; that you use the twenty-five dollars you have received as a retainer, and that you tell him you understand a man has been found murdered in your apartment in Los Angeles. You ask him to get in touch with the police and see if they want to interrogate you.'

She said, 'Collin Durant was playing his cards close to his chest. He told me that Mr Olney's picture was a fake – to tell Rankin. Then, after I'd told Mr Rankin, he said that was exactly what he'd wanted me to do.'

'Did he tell you why he wanted you to tell Rankin?'

'He said he was laying for Mr Rankin.'

'And that he wanted Rankin to sue him?'

'Not in so many words. He just said he was laying for Rankin.'

'Not Olney?'

'No, just Rankin. Then he came to me and told me that I had to get out fast. He said I had an hour but that I was to walk out casually without taking even so much as a toothbrush. He said he'd meet me at the bus terminal before eight o'clock if he didn't get back to the apartment before I left. He said I was to go to Mexico, that I could stay in Acapulco if I wanted, but that I had to take the bus to El Paso, and then go on down to Mexico City.'

'Did he have a key to your apartment?'

'Not that way. He had one last night. He made me give him one of mine.'

'Last night?'

'Yes. I had two keys. I gave him one and then later I gave Miss Street the other.'

'Why did he want one of your keys if you were leaving?'

91

'He said he was going to check the apartment and make certain I hadn't left any notes or made it seem I'd skipped out. He said I was to take just the clothes I was wearing, no suitcase, nothing. I was just to walk out – casually.

'He seemed particularly afraid someone would see me leaving carrying a suitcase. He felt detectives might be keeping an eye on me.'

Mason shook his head. 'It won't work, Maxine. That story won't stand up. Go to a lawyer here. Then you ring up your sister and see if she and your brother-in-law will stand back of you and . . .'

Mason broke off at the expression on Maxine's face.

'You mean they wouldn't?' Mason asked.

'Oh, my God,' she said, 'I can't. I simply can't.'

'Can't what?'

'Can't let them get dragged into it.'

'Dragged into it?' Mason said. 'To the extent that they are relatives of yours and that you were on your way to join them, they're already in it.'

'I wasn't . . . I wasn't going to join them. I was just going to explain things to them and get money enough to keep on going up to Canada or someplace where no one could find me – only I intended to tell them I'd keep in touch with them and if Collin Durant wanted to know where I was I'd tell him where he could get in touch with me. . . . I wouldn't bring trouble to their house. I wouldn't—'

'Don't try to lie to me,' Mason said, 'at least in such a bungling manner. You were streaking your way up the coast in order to be with them. You sent your sister a wire to send you money. It was just the amount of money you needed to get food for yourself and gas for the car in order to get up there.'

Maxine slid over into the corner, put her head up against the wall of the booth, and closed her eyes wearily.

'I give up,' she said at length. 'I can't convince you and I'm telling you the truth. . . . I'm so darned tired!'

'Want to make a confession?' Mason asked. 'And remember, Maxine, I'm not your lawyer. Anything you tell me won't be confidential.'

'Mr Mason, you've got to help me.'

'I can't help you.'

'Why not?'

'I have other interests.'

'In the— You mean with Mr Rankin?'

'Yes.'

She shook her head and said, 'Rankin has nothing to do with this.'

'I can't help you,' Mason said, 'at least not without his permission.'

She kept her eyes closed, kept herself propped in the corner of the booth. 'I give in, Mr Mason,' she said. 'I'll tell you what Durant had on me.

'My sister married Homer Stigler. That was years ago. He went overseas in the army. While he was away she met someone who had a glib line of chatter and it all happened at a time when her marriage was just about ready to break up.

'Homer had been gallivanting around a little bit overseas and Phoebe had heard about it. She decided the marriage was on the rocks, but she didn't write him one of the "Dear John's" letters because she had heard so much about those and how they disrupted morale in the armed services. She thought she would just carry on until he came back and then she'd tell him. Or she'd let him make the first move.

'So the next thing Phoebe knew she was pregnant and then things dragged along for a while and then just before the baby was born she got a letter from Homer stating that he'd made a fool of himself, that he'd been tangled up with this girl overseas but that it was simply one of those physical affairs that happen when a man is kept away from home and is hungry for feminine companionship and he begged forgiveness and told her that he would be home in six months and wanted to begin all over again and that she was the only woman he had ever really loved.

'By the time Phoebe had found out that this man she had been interested in was just a playboy and a heel. As soon as he found out about her condition, he had dropped her like a hot potato.

'Phoebe realized she wanted to save her marriage if she could – and, well, I became the fall guy.'

'What do you mean?' Mason asked.

'She wrote him that I had had an affair, that I was going to have a baby and that she had invited me to come and live with her. And that when the baby was born we were going down to California and I could have the baby and then we'd put it out for adoption.'

'And what happened?' Mason asked.

'We went to California. Phoebe had the baby but she used my name and we got the child in one of the homes, and then Phoebe returned to Oregon, and Homer came home and they were very happy. And then Homer suggested that they adopt my baby, a little boy.

'Well, that's the situation. Homer and Phoebe adopted the baby, I signed the necessary papers, and Homer thinks I am the erring sister who had an illegitimate child. . . . And they're very very happy.'

'What would have happened if Phoebe had told him the truth at the time?' Mason asked.

'I don't know. Homer is peculiar. He's intense, he's very possessive and he's – well, he's like all men.'

'What would happen if she told him now?'

'He'd kill her and kill himself. He'd hit the ceiling. He's temperamental and— Oh, my Lord, if he ever found out now!'

'How did Durant find out?' Mason asked.

'Now, there's something,' she said. 'I don't know how he found out but he certainly made it a point to find out and he did find out. He had that secret and he held it over me. There were times when I could have killed him. He—'

'Now, wait a minute,' Mason interrupted. 'Watch your— Oh-oh!'

Maxine looked up quickly. 'What's the matter?' she asked.

'Permit me to introduce the two gentlemen who are standing behind you,' Mason said. 'One of them is Lieutenant Arthur Tragg of Homicide from Los Angeles, and I presume the other one is a member of the Redding police force.'

'Sergeant Cole Arlington of the Shasta County Sheriff's office,' Tragg said cheerfully. 'Now, what was it that you were telling Mr Mason, Miss Lindsay? Something about someone whom you could kill? Were you by any chance referring to Mr Collin Max Durant?'

'Just a minute, Maxine,' Mason said. 'I'm going to tele-

94

phone Lattimer Rankin and get his permission to represent you. For some reason I believe your story.'

'I'm glad you do,' Tragg said. 'I think the young woman probably needs an attorney. We'd like to ask her some questions.'

'Moreover,' Mason said, 'I am going to ask you not to answer any questions, not to tell the police anything, until after I have had a chance to do some checking. Then I will make a statement to the police as to your story.' Mason turned to Tragg and said, 'And I may tell you, Lieutenant, that Miss Lindsay was on the point of going to an attorney here in Redding and having him call the Los Angeles police and tell them that she had just learned the body of a man had been found in her apartment, and that she would be available for questioning.'

'How very, very nice of her,' Tragg said. 'And since she is available for questioning, perhaps she wouldn't mind coming to Headquarters and making a statement right now.'

'She was on the point of stating that she was available for questioning,' Mason said, 'but in view of what she has just told me, she is not going to make any statement to the police. I am going to investigate and make that statement for her.'

'You think she's that guilty?' Tragg asked.

'I don't think she's guilty at all,' Mason said. 'I wouldn't be representing her if I thought she was guilty. I just have the feeling that she's innocent and that there are other persons involved whose happiness requires that the information she gives to the police be restricted entirely to the matter of what happened with Collin Durant.'

'Well, of course if you adopt *that* attitude,' Tragg said, 'there's only one thing to do and that's to charge her with first-degree murder.'

'In which event,' Mason said, 'we'll demand that she be taken at once before the nearest and most accessible magistrate. Now then, if you have a warrant and want to serve it—'

'I don't have a warrant,' Tragg said. 'I want to question her.'

'Go on and question her,' Mason said.

'There's not much use doing that if she won't answer.'

95

'I'll answer.'

'I don't want your answers, I want hers.'

'Then go ahead and arrest her and we'll go to the nearest and most accessible magistrate. Give me just a minute. I want to look up some fighting trial attorney in Redding who will know the local ropes and who will back my play.'

'Now, wait a minute, wait a minute,' Tragg said, 'you're getting all out of line here. We don't want to go off half-cocked on this thing. Let's be reasonable about it.'

'How did you come up?' Mason asked. 'Chartered plane?'

'A plane that is available to us on police work of this sort,' Tragg said.

'How big a plane?'

'A twin-motored five-place plane.'

'All right,' Mason said. 'I'll make you this proposition. We'll agree to get in the plane and return to Los Angeles. I'll make statements to you on the plane as to what I know about the aspects of the case in which you're legitimately interested. When you get to Los Angeles, you can do as you see fit. You can have her indicted by the grand jury or do anything you want to, but she's not going to talk. I'm going to do the talking.'

'What's she going to do?' Tragg asked.

Mason smiled wryly and said, 'All the way back on the aeroplane this poor kid is going to get some sleep.'

Tragg pursed his lips. 'You want to telephone Rankin and get permission to represent her?' he asked.

'That's right,' Mason said. 'I want to be assured there will be no conflicting interests.'

'All right,' Tragg said. 'I want to put in a call to Hamilton Burger, the district attorney at Los Angeles, and see how he reacts to this proposition of yours. I don't think he wants to have an arrest made as yet; that is, I don't think he wants to have her definitely charged with murder and I'm damned sure he doesn't want to have her brought before a magistrate in Redding.'

'Okay,' Mason said, 'we'll declare a truce. We'll leave her with Cole Arlington provided Arlington will agree that he won't try to question her, and you and I will go put our phone calls through.'

'Let's go,' Tragg said.

They went to the phone booth. Mason called Lattimer Rankin in Los Angeles. 'Rankin,' he said, 'I've been representing you in regard to that picture of Otto Olney's. Durant has been murdered. I think they're going to charge Maxine Lindsay with the murder and I'd like to represent her if you feel there'll be no conflict of interests. But if I represent her, I'm going to be fighting for her tooth and nail.'

'Go ahead and fight for her,' Rankin said. 'She's a good kid. You say Durant was murdered?'

'That's right.'

'I hope they find the person that did it,' Rankin said, 'because he should have a medal. He—'

'Shut up!' Mason snapped. 'Someone may ask you on the witness-stand what you said when you heard that Durant had been murdered.'

'Oh, in that case,' Rankin said, 'I will testify that I said what a shame it was and how I hoped they got the person who did the killing, and that's all I'll say. However, if you want to go ahead and read my mind, Mr Mason, you're at perfect liberty to do so. And by all means, represent Maxine.'

Mason hung up, opened the door of the phone booth, grinned at Lt Tragg and said, 'Go ahead and put through your call, Lieutenant, I'll meet you at the table in the restaurant. I'm going over to see that this deputy sheriff doesn't start asking too many questions.'

CHAPTER NINE

It was nearly ten o'clock that night when Perry Mason sat down opposite Lattimer Rankin in the latter's house.

Rankin, tall, ungainly, seemed somehow ill at ease.

'I wanted to thank you for giving your consent so readily over the telephone this afternoon,' Mason said, 'permitting me to represent Maxine Lindsay.'

'I certainly see no reason why I should stand in the way,'

Rankin said, 'if you want to represent her. It came as rather a surprise to me, and of course I was completely bowled over with the news of Durant's death.'

'You seemed to be able to bear up under it,' Mason said dryly.

'Well,' Rankin said, 'I've been thinking that over and I'm a little ashamed of myself, Mason. I suppose a man shouldn't speak ill of the dead who can't defend themselves. However, the man was a terrific bounder.'

'I want to find out what you know about him,' Mason said.

'It isn't very much. He started buying and selling paintings on some kind of a commission basis and gradually pushed himself forward as an expert on art. I'll say one thing for the man, he certainly was a worker. He'd study and he'd listen, and he never seemed to forget anything he ever heard. He had the most remarkable memory I have ever encountered.'

'How did he get his clients?' Mason asked.

'I don't think he had so many clients but he was a sharp-shooter. H'd pick up paintings and he seemed to know just who would be interested in any particular painting. He understood his potential customers.'

'He was good at that phase of the business?' Mason asked.

Rankin hesitated for a long moment, then conceded somewhat grudgingly, 'Yes, he was good at that particular phase of the business. Very good.'

'And you're perfectly willing for me to represent Maxine Lindsay in this case?'

'Are they going to charge her with murder?'

'I think so, yes.'

'What evidence do they have?'

'They're not confiding in me,' Mason said. 'I do know they have some evidence that they are not disclosing to the public at the present time and I believe they've recovered the murder weapon and traced that to Maxine, that is, proved that she owned it.'

Rankin crossed his long legs and frowned.

'Of course,' Mason went on, 'if I'm representing her I have to represent her and her alone. If your general interests, for instance, should come in conflict with hers in this murder case, I'd be loyal to her interests. I'd do absolutely anything that was necessary in order to bring about her acquittal.'

'Certainly,' Rankin said. 'I would expect that.'

'For instance,' Mason went on, 'if it should turn out that you had murdered Collin Durant, I wouldn't hesitate a minute. I'd uncover that evidence and brand you as the murderer. I'd have to do that in order to be fair with my client.'

'Go right ahead, Mason,' Rankin invited. 'If you can prove I murdered the guy, you're very welcome to do so.'

He chuckled for a moment, crossed his legs again and interlaced his long, bony fingers.

'I understand,' Mason said, 'that the police found a great deal of money on Collin Durant when they found the body. I would like to know, Rankin, if you know anything about that money.'

'I don't,' Rankin said, 'and it bothers me. I happen to know that on the afternoon of the day of his death, Durant was pretty badly strapped. In fact, he rang up a friend of mine and told her he had need of a thousand dollars right then and asked her if she would either loan it to him or advance him the money on a painting he had and to which he said he had a good title.'

'What did this person tell him?' Mason asked.

'She told him no. She let him know quite definitely that she wouldn't let him have a plugged nickel.'

'Do you know how much he had on him at the time of his death?'

'I understood he had an even ten thousand dollars, all in hundred-dollar bills.'

'Yet a few hours earlier he had been trying to raise a thousand from this friend of yours?'

'Yes.'

'What time was that?'

'About five o'clock in the afternoon.'

'Then, at sometime around eight o'clock he had ten thousand dollars in hundred-dollar bills.'

'That's right. At least, that's what I understand the police found on the body, and they fix the time of his death at around eight o'clock.'

'In that event,' Mason said, 'Durant had made a raise somewhere. Someone had financed him, and he'd increased his sights so that instead of asking one thousand he was asking ten thousand.'

Rankin nodded.

'No idea where that money came from?'

Rankin shook his head.

'Let's make mighty certain of one thing, Rankin,' Mason said, 'that there's nothing about this case that you know and are concealing.'

There was a long period of rather uncomfortable silence, then again Rankin slowly shook his head. 'Nothing,' he said.

'All right, Rankin,' Mason said. 'Now tell me the name of your friend, the one Durant tried to put the bite on.'

'I prefer not to mention her name.'

'It's important.'

'To whom?'

'To Maxine Lindsay – and to you.'

'Why to me?'

'I want to know how you're mixed up in it.'

'I'm not mixed up in it.'

'You will be if you don't tell me the name of this person.'

Rankin thought things over for a while, then said, 'I never thought he'd call *her* on a thing like that. It was Corliss Kenner. He told her he was coming to see her and that he needed a thousand dollars. She called me and told me.'

'What did she tell him?'

'You want to know?'

'Yes.'

'Told him to go to hell.'

Mason frowned, abruptly arose from his chair.

'I'm just running down all the angles,' he said, 'and I wanted to be sure that there was no misunderstanding between us.'

'There isn't,' Rankin told him. 'I understand your position and respect it. No matter what happens, don't pull any punches – don't pull any punches.'

'I won't,' Mason assured him. 'I'm not much of a punch-puller.'

CHAPTER TEN

It was after eleven o'clock when Mason fitted his latchkey to the exit door of his private office, swung open the door and found the lights on.

'Hi, Della,' Mason said. 'What are *you* doing around here this time of night?'

'Waiting for you,' she said, smiling. 'How was the trip?'

'Well, I guess you know just about everything I know. We caught up with Maxine, the police caught up with her, I got Rankin's permission to represent her, and I'm stuck with her.'

'Why did you decide to represent her, Chief?'

'I'm darned if I know,' Mason said, 'except that I think the kid was telling the truth and if she is, she made quite a sacrifice for someone she loves. And if she's that kind of a girl I thought she was entitled to the breaks.'

'Well,' she said, 'Paul Drake has been having kittens for the last half-hour. He wants you to get in touch with him the minute you come in. You didn't stop by his office?'

'No,' Mason said, grinning. 'I had an idea you *might* be here and I thought I'd come on down and see you first. Give Paul a ring and tell him I'm home.'

Della Street whirled the dial of the telephone and in a moment she said, 'Hi, Paul. He's home. . . . Okay, we'll be waiting.'

Della Street hung up and said, 'He's on his way down here. He's struck pay dirt somewhere along the line.'

Della Street walked over to stand by the corridor door so that the minute Drake's code knock sounded on the panel she could open the door.

Drake, his face grey with fatigue, tired pouches under his eyes, said, 'Hi, folks. . . . Gosh, I'm glad you're back, Perry. . . . If I don't get some sleep tonight I'm going to fall on my face. But I've got something I thought you should know about.'

'What?'

'Durant was in the business of making and selling phoney

pictures. He had a very gifted copyist who could just about copy any painting that you'd put in front of him. The guy has no particular originality but he is a demon as a copyist.'

'How do you know all this?'

'I know the guy,' Drake said.

'How did you get in touch with him, Paul?'

'It's a long story,' Drake said. 'I started running down everything I could get on Durant, and I found that there's an art store here that gave Durant quite a charge account and had been holding the bag for a large part of the balance due.

'So naturally I started wondering why Durant would be buying canvases and paints and brushes and painters' supplies and so forth, and so I went down and had a talk with the art store. I intimated that I might be able to dig up some information that would help him get the bill paid up, and learned that the supplies had all been delivered to one address – a sort of a beatnik studio – a chap by the name of Goring Gilbert, who signed receipts for the material – and all of a sudden Durant's credit was good as gold again.'

'You've talked with Gilbert?' Mason asked.

'No, I haven't, but I've checked on him and find that he's a very expert copyist and has a whale of a lot of talent. Some of his copies have been hung as originals. That is, the guy can copy the style of any given painter. If you'll give him a picture, say a big coloured photograph made by the dye-transfer process or a calendar picture or something of that sort, and tell him to imitate the style of some famous artist, the guy can do it well enough so that at times it fools even the experts – or at least that's what *he* claims.

'He's a typical beatnik, apparently, but he's rolling in dough which is something most of them don't have. That is, he's supposed to be loaded to the extent of being able to get what he wants.

'Now, here's the funny thing, Perry. Two weeks ago Durant paid off his account at the art store – with hundred-dollar bills. Now, remember that when Durant's body was found there was ten thousand dollars in hundred-dollar bills and about twenty-five dollars in smaller stuff.'

Mason said, 'What about this man, Gilbert, can we get him tonight? It's pretty late.'

Drake said, 'Sure, we can get him tonight, if you feel you have to see him right away. I've got a man riding herd on him and this is just the shank of the evening for those guys.'

'Let's go,' Mason said. 'Let's try and beat the police to it for once.'

'How about me?' Della Street asked.

'You go home,' Mason said, 'and get some sleep.'

Drake said, 'This is a dump, Della. It's not for nice girls.'

'Phooey to you, Paul Drake,' she said. 'You've whetted my curiosity. I'm not going to sit up here doing all the chores and then when the party gets spicy have you bundle me up and send me home.'

'These people are far out,' Drake said. 'The women are artists and models who are – well, they think nothing of posing in the nude.'

'I've seen nudes before,' Della Street said, and then added shyly, 'and how about you, Mr Paul Drake?'

Mason grinned. 'Come on, Della, if you want. Bring some notebooks and let's go.'

'Your car or mine?' Drake asked.

'Yours,' Mason said. 'I'll relax and let you worry about the traffic signals and the tickets, if any.'

'There won't be any,' Drake said. 'I'm a chastened guy. I had the job of investigating an automobile accident about two weeks ago, and in case you don't know, I've completely and utterly reformed. After you see people strewn around the road the way I saw them – well, it gives you something to think about, and I mean think.'

'Good,' Mason said. 'I got cured a while ago. The Traffic Safety Editor of the *Deseret News and Telegram* in Salt Lake City took me to task for my fast driving. Now I'm glad to see you've reformed. You can chauffeur me from now on – until you start getting reckless again. Come on, Della.'

They left Mason's office, went to the parking lot, and Drake drove them to a so-called apartment building, a combination of studios and living quarters. The building had evidently been used at one time as a warehouse. The elevator was a huge, slow-moving affair which inched its way upward carrying Mason, Della Street, and Paul Drake to the third floor.

Drake located the apartment of Goring Gilbert and knocked on the door. When there was no answer he pounded with full knuckles, then turned to Mason, shrugged his shoulders, and said, 'Nobody home.'

'Is the door locked?' Della Street asked.

Drake hesitated, said in a low voice, 'I have an operative around here somewhere, Perry. He'll know where the guy is. All we need to do is to—'

A door across the corridor opened. A woman somewhere in her late thirties or early forties, heavily fleshed, wearing nothing except a light robe stood in the doorway, a cigarette dangling pendulously from a flabby lower lip.

'Something?' she asked, her eyes impudently curious as she surveyed the group.

'Goring Gilbert.'

'Try thirty-four,' the woman said. 'There's a party down there.'

'Which direction?' Mason asked.

The woman jerked with her thumb.

As the trio moved off down the corridor, the woman stood in the doorway watching.

Hi-fi music seeped its way through the door of Studio 34.

Drake's knuckles gave a loud knock.

The door was opened by a slender, trim-figured young woman in a bikini bathing suit, who said, 'Well, come on—'

She stopped mid-sentence as she surveyed the group, then said over her shoulder, 'Okay, Goring, I guess it's for you. Outsiders.'

A man attired in a sport shirt which was unbuttoned, a pair of slacks and apparently nothing else, came in bare-footed silence to the door, surveyed the party.

'Goring Gilbert?' Mason asked.

'That's right.'

'We'd like to talk with you.'

'What about?'

'A matter of business.'

'What kind of business?'

'A painting.'

'A duplicate painting,' Drake said.

Gilbert called over his shoulder, 'See you later, folks.'

A man's voice said, 'Play it cool, man.'

Gilbert stepped out into the hall. 'My pad's down the hall,' he said.

'I know,' Mason told him.

Gilbert surveyed him. 'That's right, you would. Okay, let's go.'

He led the way down the corridor, walking with long, easy strides. His uninhibited hip motion indicated that walking barefoot was no novelty to him.

He took a key from his pocket, fitted it to the lock, twisted the knob, said, 'Come on in.'

The place was a litter of canvases, brushes, two or three easels, and smelled of paint.

'This is a working man's shop,' Gilbert said.

'I see,' Mason said.

'All right, what's worrying you cats?'

'You know Collin Durant?' Drake asked.

'Did know him,' Gilbert said. 'The guy's dead and I hope you're not trying some of this crude stuff of trying to say "How did you know he was dead unless you killed him?" – I didn't kill him, I heard it on the radio; that is, I didn't hear it but my chick did, and made me wise. Now what do *you* want?'

'You did work for Durant,' Drake said.

'What if I did?'

'Some of those paintings were forgeries that he palmed off as originals.'

'Now, wait a minute,' Gilbert said. 'What do you mean forgeries? I don't give a damn what a guy does with a painting after I sell it to him, but that guy never palmed off anything of mine that way. He always told the customer, "I have a painting which almost any expert will pronounce a genuine so-and-so. I don't think it is, but it's a swell conversation piece and I can get it for you for peanuts."

'Now, what's wrong with that?

'Soon as I heard of the murder I figured guys like you would be down here prying. Now I've told you what I know, and that's all I know.'

Mason, who had been carefully watching Gilbert, said, 'You did a certain painting that we're interested in. It was a copy job. I'm not saying it was a forgery. I simply say that it was a clever copy.'

'That's better,' Gilbert said.

'The copy,' Mason said, 'was of a Phellipe Feteet. It was a copy of a picture of women under a tree with a strongly lighted background—'

'Sure,' Gilbert said. 'All Feteet's pictures were like that.'

'Now,' Mason said, 'we want to know when you made this copy, what happened to it, and how much you were paid for it.'

Drake's face showed some surprise as he followed the lawyer's questioning.

'You got a right to ask?' Gilbert inquired.

'I've got a right to ask,' Mason said.

'Credentials?'

Mason said, 'Drake's a private detective, I'm an attorney.'

'A private detective doesn't rank and I don't have to talk to an attorney.'

'Yes, you do,' Mason said, smiling. 'You don't have to do it now but you would have to do it under oath and on the witness-stand.'

'So you want me to talk now?'

'I want you to talk now.'

Gilbert thought for a moment, then padded his way across the floor to a place where several canvases were piled up, selected the bottom canvas, pulled it out.

'This answer your question?' he inquired.

Mason and Della Street stood speechless, impressed by the sheer brilliance and artistry of the canvas; a canvas which seemed an exact duplicate of the one they had seen on Otto Olney's yacht; a canvas that had power and vivid colouring. The smooth texture of the skin on the women's necks and shoulders was such that one could see the sheen of light caressing the velvety softness.

'That's the one,' Mason said. 'Where did you copy it?'

'Right here in the studio.'

'You had the original to copy from?'

'My methods are none of your damned business. I did it, that's all. It's a hell of a good job and I'm proud of it. It's got everything that Phellipe Feteet ever had. Those were my in-

106

structions, to make a copy so accurate you couldn't tell it from the original.'

'How in the world did you do it?' Della Street asked.

'That's my secret,' Gilbert said. He turned back to Mason. 'Now, what about it?'

'How long ago did you do it?'

'Couple of weeks ago, and it took me a while – the way I work.'

'Slow?' Mason asked.

'Spasmodic,' Gilbert said.

'How much were you paid for it?'

'I'll answer that on the witness-stand, if I have to.'

'You're going to have to,' Mason said, 'and if you answer it now, it might save a lot of trouble. I'd particularly want to know whether Durant paid you by cheque.'

'No cheques,' Gilbert said. 'Durant, you say? That guy! Look, you've got all the information now you're going to get, so I'm going back to my party and you're going back to yours.'

Della Street said, 'Would you answer one question for me, Mr Gilbert?'

Gilbert turned and surveyed her from head to foot. His face showed approval. 'For you, baby, yes, I'd answer one question for you.'

'Were you paid for that picture in hundred-dollar bills?' Della Street asked.

Gilbert hesitated a moment, then said, 'I wish you hadn't asked me that question, but I told you I'd answer your question and I'll answer it. Yes, I was paid in hundred-dollar bills and since you I like I'll tell you the rest of it. It was an even two thousand and I had it in twenty one-hundred-dollar bills, and it has nothing to do with what you're after.'

'Two weeks ago?' Mason asked.

'About that, when I got paid. About ten days.'

'How did you get the painting back?' Mason asked.

'No one ever took it. It was left here.'

'Any marking on that picture so you can identify it in case the question should arise as to whether this is the copy or the original?'

'I can tell,' Gilbert said, 'and I'll bet nobody else can.'

'Are you certain this is the copy?'

'It's the copy.'

Mason said, 'What will you take for it?'

'You mean you want to buy it?'

'I might.'

Gilbert said, 'Don't crowd me. I'll think it over and let you know.'

'When?'

'When I make up my mind.'

Mason said, 'Here's one of my cards. 'I'm Perry Mason, the lawyer.'

'Hell, I know,' Gilbert said. 'I recognized your face when I saw you standing there. You've been photographed too much . . . . Who's the chick?'

'Della Street, my secretary,' Mason said.

Gilbert's eyes went over her again. 'Crazy,' he said.

'Thanks,' Della Street said.

'What are you doing now?' Gilbert asked. 'Business or pleasure?'

'Business.'

'When do you get off?'

Della Street surveyed him. 'Any time.'

'Want to ditch these squares and come on down to a party – nice people, no hypocrisy, no detours, no yakkity-yak; talk straight from the shoulder?'

'Some other time, maybe,' Della Street said. 'Do you have the right to sell this painting?'

'How should I know?' Gilbert asked. 'If I sold it to a lawyer, he could worry about the title.'

Mason said, 'It may be very important to make certain that nothing happens to that picture. Just how much money would you want for it right now so I could take it out of here with me?'

Gilbert said, 'Money, money, money! I get so damned tired of square talk about money, I could scream!

'You know something? That's my trouble. I've got talent that people want to buy for money, and I'm so damned screwy that I take the money. Now, I'm going to tell you something, Mr Perry Mason. I don't want money. I've got money. I've got enough to pay the rent on this pad, I've got enough to buy food, I've got enough to buy juice. Everything else I get for nothing.

'You know something? I was just on the point of *giving* that painting to your secretary just so she would have something to remember me by, but now I think I'll hang on to it for a while.

'I'll tell you something else. Don't ever come down here and start offering me money. I'm finished with money. I am getting so I'm becoming a square myself. Money can't live your life for you. Money can only give you a lot of false objectives. You can't *buy* your way to happiness. You can only *live* your way to happiness.

'I think your chick's all right, but you two are in a rut. The sad part of it is you have brains enough to break away from the routine if you'd just give yourselves a break, but you don't have guts enough to do it; you're all wrapped up in the conventions. To hell with it! I'm going back to my party and people who talk my language. Goodnight to all of you. Come on, I'm closing up the joint.'

'I want to be sure that nothing happens to that painting,' Mason repeated. 'It may be important.'

'Your needle's stuck,' Gilbert said. 'You've been all over that before. You're wearing out the record.'

'I just wanted to be sure I was registering on your wavelength,' Mason told him.

'You're coming in loud and clear. I heard you the first time and the second time. Now, don't waste any more of my time and don't offer me money. I'm sick of money.'

He looked Della over again. 'Come back anytime, Sugar.' Then to Mason and Paul Drake, 'Okay. I'm going back to the party. Come on, you guys are out.'

They walked out into the hall. Gilbert pulled the door shut. The spring lock clicked into place.

'Have fun,' Della Street said.

He turned, looked her over, then said, '*We* do. *You* could.'

He stood with them for a half-moment at the elevator, then barefooted his way on down the corridor.

'There's a man who has talent, remarkable talent,' Mason said. Then he turned to Della Street. 'How did you know Durant paid for the duplicate painting in hundred-dollar bills?'

'I didn't,' she said. 'I just made a shot in the dark.'

'You hit quite a bull's-eye,' Mason said.

'Do you suppose they arranged things so that duplicate picture was actually hung in the saloon in the yacht?' Drake asked.

'No,' Mason said. 'They weren't ready to switch paintings until after Olney had taken the bait. They needled Olney and Rankin, knowing someone would fall for it and walk into the trap. After Olney had filed his suit and had his experts all ready to go on the stand and swear that the picture was genuine, if he could have arranged it, Durant would have had the duplicate substituted, so that it was the duplicate that was brought into court.

'The experts, having seen and appraised the original, would be lulled into a false security, would get up on the stand and swear that this was an original Feteet. Then Durant's attorney would have asked them to take a closer look and started cross-examining them. Suddenly the experts would have become just a little dubious and started looking for tell-tale marks of identification and perhaps not find them. They might have either continued to swear that it was an original or they might have backed up on their opinion and become more or less panic-stricken. Durant would have won out in either event.'

'But could he have proved that it was a copy?' Drake asked.

'They've got some secret mark on it, something that would have enabled him to *prove* it was a copy; that is, there's some way of proving it was painted years after Feteet's death.'

'Then, if he'd lived, Durant would have been able to have taken Olney for quite a ride.'

'If he'd lived,' Mason said dryly.

'So now?' Drake asked.

'Now,' Mason said, 'you'd better keep your men working but go get yourself a night's sleep, Paul. You look tired.'

'The reason I look tired,' Drake said, 'is because I am tired. For your information, I'm going to stumble into a Turkish bath and sweat a lot of fatigue poisons out of me. Then I'm going to hit the hay and it's going to be someplace where you can't reach me on a telephone. Tomorrow morning I'll be back on the job. Tonight I'm bushed, finished, all in, down and out, and I'm not going to get back on the job no matter what happens.'

'Tomorrow,' Mason said, 'you'll be like a new man.'

'Tomorrow is a long way off,' Drake told him.

'And tomorrow you'll cover the banks?'

'What about the banks?'

'Where,' Mason asked, 'does a man get hundred-dollar bills?'

'I don't know,' Drake said. 'I wish I did. I could use some.'

'From banks,' Mason told him. 'You don't go into a store and say, "May I cash a cheque and would you give it to me in hundreds, please?" You don't go to a motion picture theatre and slide a thousand-dollar bill under the wicket and say, "Please give me the change in hundreds." '

Drake blinked thoughtfully.

'Durant,' Mason went on, 'had no bank account that meant anything. He couldn't pay his rent. He was in debt. He bought painters' supplies and ran behind. Then he paid off with hundred-dollar bills. That was two weeks ago. He had painting supplies sent to a beatnik artist. He paid the artist in hundred-dollar bills. Then he was broke again. Then he wanted Maxine out of town. He didn't have any money to give her. He went away. He came back. He had hundred-dollar bills.'

'You mean he had another bank account under an assumed name?' Drake asked.

'The banks were closed,' Mason said.

'I'm tired,' Drake told him. 'I don't want to cope with it.'

'Go get a Turkish bath,' Mason told him, 'and you can cope tomorrow.'

The lawyer turned to Della Street. 'I'm taking you home, Della, and tomorrow at eight-thirty we have a conference in the office.'

'Nine-thirty,' Drake said.

'Eight-thirty,' Mason repeated.

'Nine.'

'Eight-thirty.'

'All right,' Drake said. 'Eight-thirty. What's an hour out of a night's sleep?'

CHAPTER ELEVEN

Mason opened the door of his office promptly at eight-thirty.

Della Street evidently had been there for some time. The electric coffee percolator had filled the room with the aroma of coffee.

As Mason walked in, Della Street smiled a greeting, turned the spigot and filled a cup with steaming coffee.

'Paul?' Mason asked.

She shook her head. 'Not at his office yet and he hasn't shown.'

Mason looked at his watch, frowned.

Abruptly Drake's code knock sounded on the door.

Mason indicated the coffee percolator to Della, said, 'I'll open the door.'

The lawyer opened the door. Drake entered and almost mechanically extended his hand as Della Street put the cup and saucer in it.

'Now, *that's* service!' Drake said.

'Up and at 'em, Paul,' Mason told him. 'This is the day you're going to have to cope.'

'What do we cope with?' Drake asked.

'Police,' Mason said. 'We have to know how much of a case they have against Maxine. There's something they're not releasing. We have to find out about Collin Durant's hundred-dollar bills. When he needed money bad enough he could get it, in hundred-dollar bills. But he had to need it for some dire business necessity. For personal expenses such as paying his rent, he didn't have money.'

'He had it all right,' Drake said, 'but he wasn't putting out. He had it stashed away somewhere. When you get hundred-dollar bills after the banks close, you have the money cached away somewhere.'

'Ten thousand bucks?' Mason asked.

Drake sipped the coffee, said after a moment, 'He was going places. He had cleaned out his whole hiding-place.'

'All right,' Mason said, 'try and find it.'

'I can help you on the police end,' Drake said after a moment.

'How come?'

'I stopped by the office. One of my men had a report. He'd talked with a newspaper reporter. They had Maxine in a show-up box. Some woman identified her absolutely and positively. The police were tickled to death.'

Mason put down his coffee cup, started pacing the room.

Paul Drake held out his empty coffee cup. Della Street filled it.

'They aren't taking her before a grand jury,' Drake said. 'They're going to file a complaint and have her bound over for trial and prosecute the case by information.'

'Where did you get all this?' Mason asked.

'My operatives were working all night,' Drake said. 'I haven't had a chance to do more than skim through the reports. I took a quick look and then came on in here.'

Mason picked up his briefcase. 'I'm going down to have a talk with Maxine,' he said.

'Want me with you?' Della Street asked.

Mason shook his head. 'I'm going to talk with her and see at what point she starts lying. She'd be more cautious with another woman present. I want to have her turn on the charm and try to make a believer out of me.'

'She's already done that or you wouldn't have taken the case,' Drake said.

'I know,' Mason said. 'I felt that way yesterday. Today I need a little reassurance.'

'You'll fall for her all over again, hook, line, and sinker,' Drake said.

'I hope I do,' Mason told him. 'If she can sell her story to me the way I feel this morning, she can sell it to a jury.'

Della Street said, 'Don't be a square, Paul. That's why he's going to see the girl.'

'Oh, Lord,' Drake moaned. 'You picked up the jargon last night. I'm a square!'

The phone rang. Della Street picked up the receiver, said to the switchboard operator, 'What is it, Gertie?'

She reached hurriedly for a pencil, made shorthand notes, asked, 'Is that all?' and hung up.

113

She turned to Mason.

'A wire from George Lathan Howell, consulting art expert. He asks you to convey his undying affection to Maxine and says he is sending you his cheque for two thousand dollars as his campaign contribution.'

Drake whistled. 'That girl,' he announced, '*has* something! When do I get to meet her, Perry?'

The lawyer grinned. 'Whenever you make a two-thousand-dollar campaign contribution, Paul.'

CHAPTER TWELVE

Maxine said tearfully, 'I've followed your instructions. Mr Mason. I haven't talked and it's been very, very hard.'

'Have they used any third-degree stuff?' Mason asked. 'Did they keep you up all night?'

'No, not that. They let me get to sleep about midnight. But the newspapers were the bad ones.'

'I know,' Mason said. 'Told you that the worst thing you could do was to keep silent; that if you'd give them a break and give them an interview, they'd handle it in such a way that it would arouse public sympathy; that if you didn't give them a story, the only thing they could do was to describe you in a way that would alienate the public.'

'How did you know?' she asked.

'It's the standard line,' Mason told her. 'But I don't want you making any statement until I've had a chance to check what information the police have.'

'What difference does that make?'

'It makes this difference,' Mason said. 'Many and many a person would have gone scot-free if he hadn't started lying about something that was completely non-essential. The police couldn't prove the suspect was guilty of the crime but they could prove the suspect guilty of lying and then the person went all to pieces.'

'I'm not going to lie.'

'What about your canary?' Mason asked.

'I had one,' she said. 'I want to know what happened to him. I tell you, I had a pet canary.'

'See what I mean?' Mason said.

'No, I don't,' she told him indignantly.

'And,' Mason went on, 'a lot depends on what the evidence shows as to the time of the murder. They'll do everything in their power to influence the pathologist to fix the time of death as early as possible.

'Now, you're going to have to help me, Maxine. You say you went to the bus station, phoned Paul Drake's office, left word with him and then waited there.'

She nodded.

'Think,' Mason said. 'Try and remember some of the people who were there. You are an attractive girl. You were hanging around the telephone waiting for a call. You were nervous. People would size you up.

'There'd probably be a wolf who was wondering if he could offer a little sympathy and make a pitch. There was probably a matronly woman who wondered if she should go over and give you a pat on the back.'

'But what good would all that do?' Maxine asked. 'Even if they saw me.'

'If they saw you,' Mason said, 'and you can describe them, we'd go to the ticket sellers at the bus depot and describe these people and see if we could find out where they went, what city they were visiting. Then we'd put ads in the paper there. We'd find out what buses left at about the hours you saw these people and talk with the bus drivers. We might – we just *might* get a lead.'

Maxine said, 'I didn't notice anybody. I was upset.'

'Didn't notice anybody at all?' Mason asked.

'No.'

'How long were you there before I talked with you?'

'About an hour.'

'What time did you get there?'

'As nearly as I can tell, seven-fifteen.'

'And you didn't notice anybody?'

She shook her head.

Mason said suddenly, 'How well do you know George Lathan Howell?'

'I answered that question once,' she said.

'When?'

'When you were asking me about . . . romantic interludes, in your office.'

'I didn't mean it exactly that way this time,' Mason said. 'What I want to know now is whether there's any chance he might be mixed up in this case in some way.'

'I wouldn't know,' she said. 'Frankly, he has asked me to marry him.'

Mason said, 'He sent me a wire saying he was making a two-thousand-dollar campaign contribution.'

'Two thousand dollars!' she exclaimed.

Mason nodded.

'That means he must have sold his car and borrowed all he could.'

'He loves you that much?' 'Mason asked.

'Apparently,' she said thoughtfully.

'All right, Maxine, this is once you mustn't lie to me. Did he have a key to your apartment?'

She met his eye. 'No.'

'But Durant did?'

'I gave him one – he demanded it that night.'

Mason regarded her thoughtfully. 'You're sure he hadn't had it for some time and your present story isn't so you can account for the key to your apartment the police found on his key-ring?'

'Mr Mason, I'm telling you the truth.'

'Let's hope you are,' he said.

'I am.'

Mason said, 'All right. I'll rely on that. Heaven help you if you're not telling me the *whole* truth.

'There's going to be a preliminary hearing. I can cross-examine their witnesses. We don't have any case to put on. They'll have enough case to bind you over for trial – unless something happens and I can upset their apple-cart. They have a case against you but I don't know how much of a case. I don't want *you* to make it any stronger than it is right now. . . . And remember this. If they can prove that you *weren't* hang-

116

ing around at the telephone there at the bus depot, if they can prove that you left your apartment later than seven-fifteen, then you're in big trouble.'

She nodded.

'You told them what time you left your apartment?' Mason asked.

'Yes,' she said. 'I told them that much. I told them that I left the apartment at seven, that I didn't go back, that I phoned you from the bus depot. I told them that I met you and Miss Street, that I couldn't tell them any more without your permission – and, of course, I told them I wasn't running away, that I was just going to visit relatives; then after they found out about my sister I admitted she was the one I was intending to visit.

'But I didn't tell them anything about the case – you know, about the painting or the hold Collin Durant had on me.'

'Okay,' Mason said. 'These preliminary hearings are pretty much a matter of routine. The judge will bind you over because the evidence will be all one way. You can't get on the stand and tell your story.'

'I can't?' she asked incredulously. 'I thought I had that right.'

Mason shook his head.

'But I have to, Mr Mason. I have to go on the witness-stand. I know they'll cross-examine me. I know it will be an ordeal. I know they'll bring out things that were in my past. I know they'll do everything they can to discredit me. But I simply *have* to tell *my* story.'

'Not at the preliminary examination,' Mason said. 'You keep mum as a clam.'

'But why?'

'Because in the first place,' Mason said, 'it won't do any good. If I can beat the case, I'll have to do it by showing that the prosecution hasn't made out a case. It isn't going to do any good to establish a conflict in the evidence.

'Once the judge binds you over and you get into the Superior Court in front of a jury, then the jurors listen to your story and listen to the prosecution's witnesses and try to decide who's telling the truth. But in a preliminary examination the judge doesn't bother to resolve conflicts of evidence. He

117

figures that's up to the jury later on and in another court. If the prosecution puts on any case at all, that's all there is to it.'

'All right,' Maxine said at length, 'I guess I can take it if I have to. You're the one who tells me what to do.'

Mason regarded her thoughtfully. 'I have a feeling,' he said, 'that you didn't kill him. I also have a feeling that you're holding out something. However, I'm going to know a lot more about the case and a lot more about you by the time we get finished with that preliminary hearing.'

'When will it be?' she asked.

'Within the next couple of days,' Mason said. 'I want to find out what evidence they have. Then I'll know more about the case.'

'Do they put on all their evidence?'

Mason said, 'They try to hold out as much as they can, but my job is to needle them into putting on their whole case. . . . Sit tight now. Tell the newspaper people that you'll give them your story just as soon as I give you an okay. In the meantime, don't say anything to anyone. Don't do anything that would give the prosecution any ammunition.'

CHAPTER THIRTEEN

Paul Drake, perched on the rounded arm of the client's over-stuffed leather chair, said, 'Why don't you get rid of this thing, Perry?'

'What thing?'

'This chair.'

'What's wrong with it?'

'It's old-fashioned. It's out of style. Modern law offices don't have these things any more.'

'I have it,' Mason said.

'Why?'

'It makes the client feel comfortable. He's relaxed. He feels more at home. He's inclined to tell his story. You can't get a story out of a client who's uncomfortable – that is, if he's telling the truth.

'On the other hand, if he isn't telling the truth, I let him sit in that chair for a while and then ask him to sit in the straight-backed chair across the desk so I can hear him better. That chair is just as uncomfortable as I can make it.'

'That chair,' Drake said, 'is an invention of the devil.'

'When you want someone to tell the truth,' Mason said, 'you put them in a comfortable chair and give them every assurance of stability, sympathy, and comfort – that is, if they're co-operative.'

'And if they're not, then you put them in that uncomfortable chair?'

'That's right. The more awkward they can be made to feel, the more they have to shift their position in order to try and be comfortable. Then I let them feel they're giving themselves away by being unable to sit still. Once a man begins to shift his position and cross his legs and recross them, I look at him accusingly, as much as to say, "Aha, my lad, the falsehoods you are telling are making you uncomfortable."'

'Well,' Drake said, 'you'd better get your client, Maxine, and put her in the uncomfortable chair, Perry.'

'What's the matter?'

'She's been lying to you.'

'What about?'

'Well, let's put it this way, Perry. I don't know just what she's told you but I *think* she's been lying to you.'

'Go on,' Mason said.

'Did she tell you that she was supposed to have had a child out of wedlock, that actually it was her sister's child, that her sister had been cheating on her husband while he was overseas and that this was her sister's child?'

'Go on,' Mason said as Drake hesitated.

'Well,' Drake said, 'apparently it's the other way around. The child was Maxine's but it was agreed between her and the sister that she'd tell this cock-and-bull story about the sister having cheated on her husband. The husband knows all about it and was willing to ride along in order to cover up for Maxine.

'The child was born while the husband was overseas, all

right, but it was born to Maxine and not to the sister, Phoebe Stigler. However, Maxine and Phoebe went together down to a small community where they could say they had swopped identities. They had a midwife where the child was born, and subsequently, after a lot of legal hocus-pocus, the child was adopted by Homer and Phoebe Stigler.'

'The police know that?' Mason asked.

'Know it?' Drake said. 'Hell's bells, you haven't heard anything yet. The father of the child was Collin Max Durant.'

'What!' Mason exclaimed.

'That's what the police think. They're trying desperately to get the evidence all lined up.

'I'll tell you something else. They have a woman who knows that Maxine was in her apartment as late as eight o'clock.'

'She couldn't have been,' Mason said. 'She called you from the bus station at seven-fifteen.'

'She *said* she was calling from the bus station,' Drake said. 'That's a cheap way to get an alibi. A person goes to a telephone booth, gets the number of the phone in a far-away pay station, calls up someone who isn't in, then leaves a message saying, "I'm at such and such a number. It's a telephone booth. Please call me back." Then after she gets done committing her murder and cleaning up, she goes down to the telephone booth and waits for the call.

'Maxine Lindsay knew she was going to have to take a powder. She removed everything from her apartment that she didn't want the police to find. She also wanted her canary to have good care so she took it and left it with some very close friend. Then she got in touch with you and told you this grandstand story, gave Della Street the key to her apartment and was on her way.

'She's using you and she's using me to help build up an alibi, to confirm her story that she called from the phone booth at the bus depot.'

'How do the police figure Durant was the father of the child?'

'They figure it out on a basis of circumstantial evidence. Durant was hanging around Maxine during that time and they were pretty thick. I guess the police can dig up some registers at motels that are in the handwriting of Colin Durant.'

'Someday,' Mason said, 'I'll get a client who will tell me the truth and the surprise will knock me out. No, wait a minute, I'll put it another way. Someday we'll get a client I can believe.'

'I hate to hand you these jolts,' Drake said, 'but that's what you pay me for.'

'What about the hundred-dollar bills?' Mason asked.

'I can't find them, I can't find any indication that Durant ever had but one bank account or ever went near any other bank. I've had photographs and operatives with photographs calling on every bank in town. No one knows him except the little branch bank where he had an account under his own name. At the time of his death he had a balance of thirty-three dollars and twelve cents.'

'With ten thousand dollars in his pocket,' Mason said.

Drake nodded.

'And a week or so earlier he had hundred-dollar bills that he used to buy painting supplies and pay off the artist. How about other hundred-dollar bills, Paul?'

'Those are the only ones I could find.'

'Keep jigging,' Mason said. 'Right now you have only started.'

CHAPTER FOURTEEN

Deputy District Attorney Thomas Albert Dexter got to his feet and said, 'May it please the Court, this is the time fixed for the preliminary hearing in the case of the People of the State of California versus Maxine Lindsay. The People are ready.'

'Ready for the defendant,' Mason said.

'Very well,' Judge Crowley Madison said, with a curious and almost sympathetic glance at Maxine, 'call your witnesses, Counsellor.'

'Call Lieutenant Tragg,' Dexter said.

Lt Tragg took the stand. He had, he explained, been called

by Miss Della Street, or, that is, by someone who said she was Miss Della Street, on the morning of the 14th. He had gone to an apartment, Number 338-B, rented by Maxine Lindsay, the defendant in this case, and had there found Della Street and a body. The body had subsequently been identified as that of Collin Max Durant, an art dealer. The body was lying partially in the shower stall in the bathroom.

'You have photographs?' Dexter asked.

Tragg produced a sheaf of photographs. They were introduced in evidence, one at a time.

Tragg also produced a diagram he had made of the interior of the apartment, and that was introduced in evidence.

'And what was in the pockets of the deceased at the time you found the body, Lieutenant?'

'Some keys, including a key which opened the door of the defendant's apartment; a handkerchief, a penknife, a pack of cigarettes, a lighter, two fountain-pens, a notebook, one hundred one-hundred-dollar bills and about twenty-five dollars in smaller currency and change, making a total of ten thousand and twenty-five dollars.'

'Miss Street made a statement to you at that time?'

'Yes.'

'What did she say?'

Judge Madison said, 'This is not the best evidence. It's hearsay.'

'I know,' Dexter said, 'but since Miss Street is the secretary of Mr Perry Mason, the attorney for the defendant, I thought it might be better to bring the matter to the Court's attention in this way, particularly if there is no objection from the defence.'

'Is it material?' Judge Madison asked.

'It's quite material.'

'Is it important?'

'We consider it so.'

'In what way?'

'It tends to contradict the defendant's subsequent declarations.'

'Very well,' Judge Madison said, 'if there is no objection—'

'There is an objection,' Mason said.

'Well,' Judge Madison said irritably, 'that would have disposed of the matter without all this running around, if you had interposed the objection at the time the question was asked.'

Mason smiled. 'I am objecting at this time.'

'The objection is well taken. It's sustained,' Judge Madison said, and then added somewhat brusquely, 'I recognize your tactics, Counsellor. You wanted the district attorney's office to explain why it considered the conversation important. All right, you have that information now, you've made your objection and it's been sustained.'

'I'll call Miss Della Street to the stand at this time in order to prove the conversation,' Dexter said, 'and withdraw Lieutenant Tragg so that he can finish his testimony later.'

'Well, that's somewhat irregular,' Judge Madison said, 'but I guess it's all right. However, if Mr Mason wants to cross-examine the lieutenant on the testimony he's already given before he leaves the stand, I'll give him that privilege.'

'I'm quite willing to cross-examine him later,' Mason said.

'Very well,' Judge Madison said. 'Miss Street to the stand.'

Della Street stepped forward, held up her right hand, was sworn and took her position on the witness-stand.

'You are acquainted with the defendant, Maxine Lindsay?'

'Yes.'

'Did you know her on the evening of the thirteenth of this month?'

'I did.'

'Did you see her at that time?'

'I did.'

'Did you have a conversation with her?'

'I did.'

'What time was this?'

'It was about nine o'clock in the evening.'

'Who was present?'

'Mr Mason and myself, in addition to Maxine Lindsay.'

'What did she say? What was that conversation?'

'Just a moment,' Mason said. 'May I ask a question on *voir dire*?'

'Certainly,' Judge Madison said.

'At the time of that conversation,' Mason said, 'what was your occupation, Miss Street?'

123

'I was your secretary.'

'And what is my occupation?'

'An attorney at law.'

Mason smiled at Judge Madison and said, 'Now, Your Honour, I wish to object to the question on the ground that it calls for a privileged communication, a confidential communication made to an attorney.'

'Just a moment,' Dexter said angrily. 'I have one more question. Miss Street, at the time of this conversation, was Maxine Lindsay a client of Perry Mason?'

Della Street hesitated. 'I don't know,' she said.

'Let me put it this way,' Dexter said. 'Had she paid any retainer?'

'She had not paid a retainer,' Della Street said.

Dexter smiled triumphantly. 'There you are, Your Honour. It was not an attorney-and-client relationship.'

'I'd like to ask a question,' Mason said. 'Is Miss Lindsay my client now, Miss Street?'

'That's self-evident,' Judge Madison interrupted. 'I don't see what that has to do with the situation. You're appearing now as attorney of record for her.'

'Then,' Mason said, 'since it is thoroughly understood that she is now my client and that I am appearing as attorney of record for her, I will ask Miss Street this question. Has she *ever* paid me a retainer?'

'No,' Della Street said, 'she hasn't.'

Judge Madison smiled. 'Pardon me, Counsellor. I didn't appreciate the drift of your cross-examination.'

Dexter said, 'I would like to ask one more question, Miss Street. Did Mr Mason tell you that he was going to represent Maxine Lindsay?'

'Yes.'

'And when did he make that statement?'

'Some time on the fourteenth.'

'Then he hadn't told you she was his client on the thirteenth?'

'He hadn't told me at that time, no.'

Judge Madison ran his hand over his head. 'I think we had better have a clearer understanding of the facts in this case,' he said, 'before the Court rules on the objection.'

Mason said, 'Permit me to ask one more question. Miss Street, was there any relationship of friendship, that is, personal friendship, between Miss Lindsay and myself, that you know of?'

'None.'

'Was there anything in this conversation to indicate that she was consulting me as a friend, rather than as an attorney?'

'No. She was consulting you because she had been in your office earlier.'

'She made that statement?'

'That was the effect of the conversation, yes.'

Mason said, 'I renew the objection, if the Court please.'

'I'm going to sustain the objection for the moment,' Judge Madison said. 'Let the evidence develop in the case. If it turns out there's enough evidence to bind the defendant over without ruling on this objection, then the prosecution can withdraw these questions because it won't be necessary to have them asked and answered.

'The Court feels there's a close point here. The Court feels that we should have some authorities on the matter, but the Court is inclined to sustain the objection.'

'Very well,' Dexter said, with poor grace. 'I'll look the matter up. I had anticipated that there would be no objection to Tragg's stating what Della Street told him. I think it's part of the *res gestae*.'

'What she told him about discovering the body might be part of the *res gestae*,' Judge Madison said, 'but what she told him as part of the conversation about what the defendant had stated the day before, or rather, the evening before, is not a part of the *res gestae*.'

'Very well, recall Lieutenant Tragg,' Dexter said.

Della Street returned to her seat.

'Lieutenant, on the afternoon of the fourteenth, did you have occasion to see Maxine Lindsay, the defendant in this case?'

'I did.'

'Where?'

'At Redding, California.'

'And who was with her at that time, if anyone?'

'Mr Perry Mason.'

'You made some statement to her at that time in the presence of Mr Perry Mason?'

'Yes, sir. I told her that I wanted to question her concerning the murder of Collin Max Durant.'

'And did she make any statement to you at that time?'

'Not at that time. Mr Perry Mason told her not to make any statement.'

'You returned to Los Angeles?'

'Yes, sir.'

'Who returned with you?'

'Mr Perry Mason and Maxine Lindsay, the defendant.'

'Subsequently Maxine Lindsay was interrogated without Perry Mason being present?'

'Yes, sir.'

'Did she make any statement?'

'At first she refused to make any statement. Then I explained to her that we didn't want to work any injustice but that there was evidence pointing to her, that if she would explain just what had happened we would investigate and if the evidence bore out her story she would be released. I then went on to tell her that the evidence of her flight was evidence which could be received as evidence of guilt in this state, and she told me that she wasn't fleeing. She said that she had decided to visit her sister, a Mrs Homer H. Stigler, who resides in Eugene, Oregon. I then asked her how long she had been on the road and learned that she had left Los Angeles at approximately nine-forty; that she was in Bakersfield a little after midnight; that she had very limited funds and that she looked around for a while getting the cheapest motel she could find.'

'You learned all this from the defendant?'

'Yes, sir.'

'She had been advised of her constitutional rights?'

'She had.'

'Then what else did she tell you?'

'That she had sent a wire to her sister asking for funds and that she had received those funds transferred by telegraph to Redding.'

'Incidentally, Lieutenant, did you talk with the sister?'

'Subsequently I talked with the sister.'

'And did the sister verify—'

'Just a minute,' Mason interposed. 'The question as now being asked is leading. Furthermore it is incompetent, irrelevant, and hearsay. The statement by the sister cannot in any way be binding on this defendant, and—'

'Withdraw the question,' Dexter said wearily. 'I was trying to save time.'

'And I was trying to preserve the constitutional rights of the defendant,' Mason said.

'Now then, subsequently did the defendant make any other statements to you?'

'Yes, she did. I suggested to her that she had arranged with Perry Mason to meet her along the road and she denied this. I then questioned her concerning the time at which she had met Perry Mason and she advised me that she had last seen Perry Mason at about nine-thirty on the evening of the thirteenth; that she had then decided to visit her sister; that she had given Miss Street the key to her apartment. I asked her how well she knew Collin Durant, the dead man, and she said at first that she barely knew him. Later on she changed her story and admitted that she had been friendly with him at one time, and that since she had been in Los Angeles she had seen him from time to time.'

'Did you ask her anything about having a child?' Dexter asked.

'Just a moment,' Mason said, 'that question is objected to as leading and suggestive. It is completely incompetent, irrelevant, and immaterial.'

'I think it is incompetent,' Judge Madison said, 'at least in its present form.'

'Well, I'll put it this way,' Dexter said bluntly. 'Did you ask her anything about having a child by the dead man, Collin Durant?'

'Not at that time, no.'

'Did you, subsequently?'

'Yes.'

'What did she say?'

'I object to this whole line of questioning as being leading and suggestive.'

'It is leading,' Judge Madison said, 'but the prosecution is trying to get some particular conversation here in evidence. I'm going to overrule the objection. I think the question is now pertinent because it would go to a question of motivation.'

'What did she say?' Dexter asked.

'She denied it.'

'Denied ever having a child, or denied that Collin Durant was the father of the child?'

'Now, just a minute,' Mason said. 'Before you answer that question I want to object, if the Court please, and I assign the asking of this question in this manner as misconduct. The Court has already ruled that the question of whether this defendant had had a child has nothing to do with the issues of this case unless the child was the offspring of Collin Durant. By approaching the subject in this manner and asking the question in this way, the prosecution is trying to put the defendant in a position where public sympathy will be alienated, where the newspapers will have a story, and—'

Judge Madison said, 'There's no need to go on, Mr Mason. The Court has already ruled on this. The Court admonishes the prosecution that the question is improper. The Court has opened the door only so far as it goes to a question whether the witness was questioned about whether she had a child by Collin Durant, and her answer to that question.'

'She denied it,' Tragg said.

'Cross-examine,' Dexter snapped.

Mason said, 'Now then, Lieutenant Tragg, did you ask her if she had had a child and the father of that child was Thomas Albert Dexter, the district attorney?'

Dexter jumped to his feet. 'Your Honour, this is ... this is rank misconduct! This is a conduct which is contemptuous on its face!'

'Why is it?' Mason asked. 'You asked the lieutenant a leading question, if he had had a conversation in which he had accused the defendant of having a child by Collin Durant. Apparently there was no foundation for any such assumption, any more than there is any foundation for the assumption that you are the father of a child by the defendant. I just wanted to drive home my point. And,' Mason added with a smile, 'in case the daily Press should regard your quote bombshell unquote as the highlight of the case, I wanted my question to illustrate my position and be a higher highlight.'

Judge Madison smiled and said, 'Proceed with some other question, Mr Mason. I think you have made your point.'

'You ascertained that the defendant did have a sister, Mrs Homer Hardin Stigler, living at Eugene, Oregon?'

'Yes, sir.'

'And that she had received a telegram from the defendant and had forwarded her twenty-five dollars in response to that message?'

'Yes, sir.'

'No further questions,' Mason said.

'One matter I overlooked,' Dexter said. 'Did the defendant tell you how she had got in touch with Mason on the evening of the thirteenth?'

'She said she had called him from a bus depot at about seven-fifteen. That she had called the office of Paul Drake and asked for Mr Mason and asked if they could get in touch with Mr Mason. She said that she waited there until about eight-fifteen and that Mr Mason called in at that time and arranged to meet her in forty-five minutes in front of the apartment building where Miss Della Street lives, and that was the reason that she met Mason and Miss Street there and gave Miss Street her key at that time.'

'You asked her other questions?'

'Yes, we asked her other questions which she refused to answer. We told her that we were making no accusations as yet, that the case was in the stage of investigation and that our questions were asked simply so she could help clear up certain matters.'

'You wish to cross-examine further?' Dexter asked.

'No further questions,' Mason said.

'I will call Dr Phillip C. Foley,' Dexter said.

Foley came forward, was sworn, and identified himself as an autopsy surgeon in the office of the county coroner.

'I will stipulate Dr Foley's professional qualifications, subject to the right of cross-examination,' Mason said. 'I wish it understood, however, that I am not stipulating to his qualifications as such, only to a prima-facie showing, and I have a right to cross-examine as to those qualifications.'

'Very well,' Judge Madison said. 'Go ahead with your questions, Mr Prosecutor.'

'I am referring to the body identified as that of Collin Max Durant, Number three, six, seven, four W in the records of the coroner's office.'

'Yes, sir.'

'Who performed the autopsy on that body?'

'I did.'

'When was it performed?'

'At approximately two o'clock on the afternoon of the fourteenth.'

'When did you first see the body?'

'At ten o'clock in the morning. Actually it was just a few minutes past ten. I would say three or four minutes past ten. It wasn't as much as five minutes past ten.'

'In your opinion, Doctor, how long had the body been dead at the time you examined it? Or, I'll put it another way: When had death occurred?'

'I would say death took place between seven-forty and eight-twenty on the night of the thirteenth.'

'Did you determine the cause of death?'

'Yes, sir. There were three bullet wounds. One of them might eventually have proven fatal. The other two would have proved instantly fatal. The bullet wound which I believe was the first wound inflicted was one which penetrated the spine at the fourth cervical. The other bullet, which I believe would have proven almost instantly fatal, penetrated the ascending aorta. The other bullet entered the lung. All three shots were fired from the back.'

'Did you recover any of the bullets?'

'I recovered all three of the bullets.'

'And what was done with those bullets?'

'I turned them over to the ballistics department for possible identification, after first labelling them so I could identify them.'

'Cross-examine.'

'The phenomenon of rigor mortis is a variable, is it not?' Mason asked.

'It is.'

'There have been instances of troops slain in the heat of

combat under circumstances of excitement and where the temperature has been high and rigor mortis has developed almost instantly?'

'I believe that is right. I have never seen that myself but I believe it is an accepted medical fact.'

'And there are circumstances under which rigor mortis is very slow in its onset?'

'Yes, sir.'

'It begins with the jaws and neck muscles and gradually works down through the body?'

'Yes, sir.'

'And when it leaves, does it leave in the same way?'

'Yes, sir.'

'Now, post-mortem lividity is also a variable, is it not?'

'Well, yes.'

'That is a phenomenon in which the forces of gravitation and those of blood deterioration or coagulation combine?'

'In a way, yes. I believe you might call it that.'

'Blood settles into the lower vessels, except where those vessels are shut off due to pressure?'

'Yes, sir.'

'The pattern is quite uniform. It follows a general pattern?'

'Yes, sir.'

'And once it has developed it does not change unless the body is moved?'

'That is right.'

'So that an autopsy expert could only tell very, very generally from post-mortem lividity what time death occurred?'

'I would say so, yes.'

'And rigor mortis is also such a variable that you can only tell very generally when death took place?'

'Yes.'

'Now in regard to body temperature, Doctor, what can you say about that?'

'Well, the body loses temperature at a uniform rate.'

'Depending, however, on the temperature of the room?'

'Yes, sir.'

'The temperature of the body at the time of death?'

'We always assume a normal temperature at the time of death in cases of this sort.'

131

'But you don't know that it exists? That's only an assumption?'

'Well, yes.'

'And the rate of loss of temperature depends on the clothing?'

'Yes, to a very large extent.'

'You didn't know the temperature of the room in which the body remained until it was removed by the police?'

'It was seventy-two degrees Fahrenheit.'

'You went to the room?'

'Yes.'

'And did what?'

'I used the newest method of ascertaining the time of death by the Lushbaugh method. By using this method incorporating an electrical direct reading thermometer with a thermistor in a plasticized probe, I was able to determine the precise rate at which body temperature was decreasing.

'This method enables one to ascertain the time of death to within thirty to forty minutes.

'I used this so-called "death thermometer" method in this case. The result agreed with all the other physical evidence I was able to evaluate and pinpointed the time of death.'

'You fix the earliest time of death as seven-forty?'

'Using this method, yes.'

'And the latest time as eight-twenty?'

'Yes.'

'Could death have occurred at seven-thirty-nine?'

'That's quibbling.'

'It could have been seven-thirty-nine?'

'Perhaps.'

'It could have been seven-thirty-eight?'

'Well, I'll put it this way, Mr Mason. I fixed those time limits as the extreme limits *under this test*. The probable time of death was midway in that period, again *under this test*.'

'That's all,' Mason said.

'Call Matilda Pender,' Dexter said.

Matilda Pender, a rather attractive woman in her early thirties was sworn, testified that she was a ticket seller at the bus depot, that she had seen Maxine Lindsay on the night of the thirteenth, that she had noticed her particularly because the girl seemed distraught and excited.

'During what time intervals did you observe her?' Dexter asked.

'Approximately between eight o'clock and eight-twenty.'

'What was she doing?'

'Standing by a telephone booth.'

'Now, did you see her before that?'

'No, sir.'

'Cross-examine,' Dexter said.

'She could have been there prior to eight o'clock without you seeing her?' Mason asked.

'I noticed her because she was nervous.'

'Exactly,' Mason said. 'If she hadn't been nervous you wouldn't have noticed her. In other words, there was nothing other than nervousness to differentiate her from the hundreds of other persons who pass through that bus depot in the course of a day.'

'Well, I noticed her because she *was* nervous.'

'I am asking you,' Mason said, 'if that was the reason you noticed her.'

'I have told you. Yes.'

'And if she hadn't been nervous, you wouldn't have noticed her.'

'No.'

'Then if she had been there prior to eight o'clock but hadn't been nervous, you wouldn't have noticed her.'

'I suppose not, no.'

'She could have been there from six o'clock and if she hadn't been nervous you wouldn't have noticed her.'

'If she'd been there that long I would have noticed her.'

'From six to eight-twenty?'

'Yes.'

'Even as it was, and she was nervous, you didn't notice her immediately, did you?'

'I suppose not.'

'So you now feel she must have been there some time before you noticed her even with all the nervousness that you have testified to.'

'I don't think she could have been there very long before eight o'clock.'

'But she must have been there before eight o'clock,' Mason said, 'because when you saw her, you saw her at the phone booth and she was nervous. You didn't see her when she entered.'

'No.'

'Then she had entered before you saw her?'

'Yes.'

'And you don't know how long before?'

'No.'

'Then if something happened to make her nervous at eight o'clock, that would account for you noticing her.'

'I noticed her because she hung around the telephone booth and acted in a nervous manner.'

'Exactly,' Mason said. 'So what you are actually testifying to is that at eight o'clock this woman became sufficiently nervous for you to notice her.'

'Yes.'

'Now, that nervousness, of course, could have been due to some telephone call that she put through, some information she received on the telephone?'

'It could have been due to anything. I'm not trying to state what caused the woman to be nervous, but only that she was nervous.'

'And because of that nervousness you noticed her?'

'Yes.'

'That's all,' Mason said.

'Call Alexander Redfield,' Dexter said.

Mason said, 'I will stipulate as to Mr Redfield that he has all of the qualifications of an expert in the field of ballistics and firearms identification, subject to my right to cross-examine. I am only making this stipulation to save time on the direct examination. I reserve the right to cross-examine as to his qualifications if I so desire.'

'Very well. We will accept that stipulation.'

Dexter turned to the witness. 'Mr Redfield, did you receive three bullets from Dr Phillip C. Foley?'

'I did.'

'And did you place those bullets where you could be certain they were not contaminated in any way?'

'I did.'

'And later on, did you compare them with a weapon for the purpose of seeing whether they had been fired from that weapon?'

'I did.'

'Can you tell us something generally about firearms identification and bullet matching?'

'Each barrel has its own peculiarities,' Redfield said. 'There are, of course, class characteristics, such as the number of lands, the pitch, the direction of the pitch, the rotation, the width and spacing. Those are what we call class characteristics. For instance, the Colt Firearms Company manufactures barrels having certain distinctive class characteristics. The Smith and Wesson barrels have entirely different class characteristics.

'In addition to these class characteristics there are also what we refer to as individual characteristics. Those individual characteristics are the result of those minute imperfections in a barrel which cause striations on a bullet which is fired through that barrel.

'Given a gun and a fatal bullet which is not too badly disfigured by impact, we are nearly always able to fire a test bullet through the gun and match it with the fatal bullet so that we can tell positively whether the fatal bullet was fired from the gun in question.'

'And you tested these bullets, which were given you, with a firearm?'

'Yes, sir, with a Hi-Standard nine-shot twenty-two revolver of the brand known as Sentinel. That is a particular brand made by the High Standard Manufacturing Corporation. The number of this particular gun was one, one, one, one, eight, eight, four. It had a nine-shot cylinder, a two and three-eighths inch barrel.'

'And what was the calibre of that gun?'

'Twenty-two.'

'What else can you tell us about that weapon?'

'It was a nine-shot revolver. Three of the chambers had been fired. There were three empty shells in the cylinder and six loaded cartridges. The gun was registered in the name of the defendant.'

'And what can you tell us about the three twenty-two calibre bullets which were handed to you by Dr Foley?'

'They had all been fired from this gun.'

'You may cross-examine,' Dexter said.

'No questions,' Mason said, smiling.

Judge Madison said, 'It now having reached the noon hour, gentlemen, Court will adjourn until one-thirty this afternoon. The defendant is remanded to custody.'

CHAPTER FIFTEEN

Mason, Della Street, and Paul Drake gathered in the little private dining-room of the restaurant near the Hall of Justice where they habitually had lunch when trying a case in court.

When they had given their orders, Mason got up and started pacing the room.

'The secret of the thing is that damned gun,' he said.

'It's Maxine's gun, all right.'

'Of course it's her gun,' Mason said. 'It's registered in her name. But there has to be something more in connection with it.'

'What more would they need?' Drake asked.

'Maxine's story,' Mason said, 'is that she kept the gun in a drawer by the bed in her apartment. Anyone who was familiar with the apartment would know where she kept the gun. Anyone could have taken the gun and committed the murder.'

'And then left the gun where?' Della Street asked.

'Presumably someplace in the apartment,' Mason said.

'But we didn't see it there,' Della pointed out. 'That is, the murderer didn't simply drop it on the floor.'

Mason nodded. 'That doesn't mean it couldn't have been there. It could have been put back in the drawer.'

'That's about the only place it could have been,' Drake said. 'If Maxine had taken it with her, she'd have told you, wouldn't she?'

'Heaven knows,' Mason said. 'You can't tell what a client will do, particularly a woman client. They get enmeshed in a

136

series of events that seem to trap them and they almost invariably try to deceive their attorneys.'

'Well,' Drake said, 'it quite definitely wasn't in her possession when she was taken into custody.'

'Suppose she'd hidden it somewhere,' Della Street said.

'Then the police wouldn't have found it at all,' Drake said. 'I don't think you have anything to worry about on the gun except the fact that it's hers, Perry. That gives the prosecution all of a case that it needs against Maxine, at least for the preliminary hearing.'

'They've got something else,' Mason said, and resumed moodily pacing the floor.

Suddenly he paused and said, 'Paul, I want you to find out if you can how often Olney has used his yacht during the past three months. I'd like to have you find out something about the caretaker system there at the yacht club; how many persons are there as caretakers or watchmen. In other words, how many people we would have to screen if we wanted to determine whether bribery had been used to get aboard the yacht. We've got to find out more about the particular bunco game that Durant was playing.'

'It seems to me it's quite simple,' Drake said. 'He gets someone to make a fake painting. Then he passes the word around that a reputable art dealer has sold a wealthy collector a fake picture. The art dealer gets mad, the man who has purchased the picture becomes furious, and they get a bunch of art experts to appraise the picture and then file suit against Durant.

'Then Durant manages to substitute the forged painting for the original. The case comes to court. Durant proves the picture is a forgery and cashes in.'

Mason resumed pacing the floor.

'You don't think so?' Drake asked.

'I don't know,' Mason said. 'He told Maxine it was a forged painting. He checked to see if she'd told Rankin that the painting was false. All of that fits into the picture – but the guy got ten thousand dollars somewhere and he told Maxine to get out of town. Now why do that?

'If the painting *hadn't* been forged, then he wanted Maxine away where no one could prove what he'd said. If he could show it *was* a forgery, then Maxine's testimony wouldn't make a particle of difference.

'The two theories are diametrically opposed in some of their aspects. Why did he want the painting forged in the first place? Why want Maxine out of town in the second place?

'There has to be something in the case we don't know, some vital factor we either don't have or are overlooking.'

Abruptly Mason turned to Paul Drake. 'Paul, hurry through your lunch. Then go up to court, get a bunch of subpoenas for the defendant and subpoena all the persons who had anything to do with that painting business. I want Otto Olney, I want that expert George Lathan Howell – and check on the records of the time the yacht has been out. See if you can find out how much of the time Olney has been there. And while you're about it, check on Olney's home life. Find out something about Mrs Olney. Serve a subpoena on her. Apparently they don't have too much in common, and Olney has been spending a lot of time on his yacht lately. While there's been no formal separation, nevertheless there's every indication his domestic relations aren't too cordial.'

The waiter brought their food.

'How about Goring Gilbert?' Drake asked. 'You want him subpoenaed?'

'I've had a *subpoena duces tecum* on him,' Mason said. 'He is directed to be there this afternoon with the forged painting.'

'That's going to cause something of a commotion?'

'I don't know. I served this *subpoena duces tecum* ordering him to appear with any painting he had painted in the style of those painted by Phellipe Feteet, and in particular any painting that showed native women gathered under a tree with kids playing in the background and sunlight on green foliage as a far background.'

'Think he'll show up?'

'If he doesn't, I'll raise such a commotion that everyone in the prosecutor's office will wish he had. I'm going to try my darnedest to get that picture into evidence.'

'Will Dexter try to keep you from getting the picture in evidence?' Della Street asked.

'He'll fight like a bronco steer,' Mason said. 'We'll have to drag him every inch of the way.'

'Why?'

'First,' Mason said, 'because he thinks it may complicate the situation and secondly because he's going to try to force me to put Maxine on the stand so that I can lay the foundation for bringing in this picture. If she testifies that Durant told her to go to Rankin and tell him about the false Feteet, then the whole thing becomes admissible. But any attorney who puts his client on the stand during a preliminary hearing in a murder case is generally considered a likely candidate for the insane asylum.

'All the defendant can do by her testimony is to raise a conflict in the evidence, and no committing magistrate is going to resolve such a conflict against the prosecution; unless, of course, it brings up a point which conclusively demolishes the whole theory of the prosecution, and the chances of doing that are just about one in ten thousand.'

'You have done it, haven't you?' Della Street asked.

'I did it in two cases,' Mason said. 'They were both extreme cases. I knew that by putting the defendant on the stand I could lay the foundation for evidence which would otherwise be inadmissible, and that evidence effectively sabotaged the prosecution's case.'

'Would you do it in this case?' Drake asked.

Mason, pacing the floor, said, 'That's what I'm trying to determine, Paul. I'm faced with a responsibility that I wish I didn't have to assume – but I'm toying with the idea right now.'

Mason went over to sit at the table, hardly eating, exploring the edges of the food with his fork, his manner preoccupied, his eyes fixed on the tablecloth.

Abruptly he pushed his plate away and got up from his chair. 'I'm going to do it,' he said.

'Do what?'

'Put her on the stand.'

Della Street started to say something, then caught herself.

'It's potential legal suicide,' Mason said. 'If it doesn't work, I'll be branded from one end of the country to the other as having made the biggest boo-boo of the year, but I'm going to do it.

'I can't get that damned picture into evidence any other way and I have to get it in before something happens to it.'

139

'What could happen to it?' Drake asked.

'Lots of things,' Mason said. 'It could disappear, it could be stolen, it could just plain be destroyed. And this man, Goring Gilbert, could just plain vanish into thin air. Who the hell's going to worry about what becomes of a beatnik painter?'

The lawyer said, 'Come on, Paul. You can get caught up on your eating sometime this evening. Right now you're going to get subpoenas served on Olney, his wife, Howell, Rankin, and the watchmen at the yacht club.'

'Why the watchmen?' Drake asked.

'I want to know when the duplicate painting was made.'

'Can you get all this in – all this properly admitted as evidence?'

'I don't know,' Mason said. 'I can sure as hell try. One thing is certain. I can have that picture so tied up that nothing is going to happen to it. I'll have it as an exhibit in court.'

'The false Feteet?' Della Street asked.

Mason nodded. 'Let's go, Paul.'

CHAPTER SIXTEEN

Promptly at one-thirty, as Judge Madison took the bench, Thomas Dexter sprang his bombshell. 'I would like to recall Matilda Pender,' he said.

The young woman returned to the stand.

'There is one more thing I want to ask you about,' Dexter said. 'You saw the defendant and she seemed nervous. She was near the telephone in the telephone booth, apparently waiting for—'

'Never mind the apparently,' Mason said, 'let's have the facts. We'll let the conclusions speak for themselves.'

'All right,' Dexter said, 'I have here a diagram of the bus terminal, showing the telephone booths, the lockers, the ticket window, the location of the rest-rooms, and the waiting-room. Also showing the doors for loading and unloading passengers. Now, will you please point out the spot on this diagram where you saw the defendant? First, however, let me ask you to orient yourself on the diagram and tell me whether or not that correctly delineates the floor plan of the premises.'

'Yes, sir. It does.'

'All right,' Dexter said, 'now let's get the defendant located as of the night of the thirteenth.'

The witness placed a pencil on the sketch.

'At about this point?' Dexter asked.

'Yes.'

'You saw her here for how long?'

'She was either there in that spot or near that spot for at least fifteen minutes that I'm certain of.'

'Then what happened?'

'Then she was in the phone booth.'

'I notice that a rack of lockers is right near the phone booths.'

'Yes, they're just behind them.'

'I'm going to ask you if you know where Locker twenty-three W is?'

'Yes, sir.'

'Where?'

'It is the third one from the top in this diagram,' she replied.

'Do you know a man by the name of Fulton – Frankline Fulton?'

'Yes, sir.'

'Did you see him either on the fourteenth or fifteenth?'

'It was the fifteenth.'

'And where did you see him, and under what circumstances?'

'I monitor the lockers at the terminal,' she said. 'Whenever one of them is unopened for twenty-four hours we check the contents, and in accordance with a notice given to the public to that effect, the contents are removed to the office and the locker is placed back in operation.'

'And how is that done?'

'Every time a coin is inserted in the locker so as to activate it,' the witness said, 'it registers on the master counter at the top of the locker. Every night before I go off work, I go through the lockers and make a list of the numbers that are shown on the master register at the top. I then compare each of these numbers with the numbers which were on the master register during the preceding twenty-four hours. Whenever I find one that is the same, I take my key and remove the entire lock.'

'You don't simply open the locker?'

'Not in that sense of the word. We take off the lock which is on there, the lock with the master register – everything. We then take whatever is in the locker out of the locker itself, put it in dead storage in the office, and put the locker back in service with a new lock and register.'

'Now on the fifteenth, did you have occasion to do that with one of these lockers?'

'Yes, sir.'

'What locker was that?'

'This locker with the number you mentioned – twenty-three W.'

'And when you took the master lock off and opened it, what did you find?'

'We found a gun.'

'Now, who was with you at the time?'

'No one at that time, but I called the police, and Frankline Fulton came right out. I believe he is a sergeant.'

'He's a member of the metropolitan police?'

'That's my understanding, yes.'

'And at his suggestion, did you make any mark on this gun so that you would know it again?'

'Yes. We both put identifying marks on it.'

'I now hand you a Hi-Standard Sentinel twenty-two calibre revolver which has previously been introduced in evidence in this case as People's Exhibit G. I ask you to look at that gun carefully and tell me if you have ever seen it before.'

The witness took the gun, turned it over in her hands, and said, 'Yes. That's the gun we found in the locker.'

'And that was the locker near which you had seen the defendant on the evening of the thirteenth?'

'Yes, sir.'

'Cross-examine,' Dexter said.

'You didn't see the defendant open that locker, did you?' Mason asked.

'No.'

'Did the police dust that locker for fingerprints?'

'Yes.'

'Was anything said to you about them?'

'Only that they found several they couldn't identify.'

Mason smiled. 'Thank you, that's all.'

'Call Agnes H. Newton,' Dexter said.

Agnes Newton had evidently spent the morning at a beauty parlour. She had selected her clothes with the hope that she would be photographed on the witness-stand, and she came forward with the manner of an opera star making her entrance on the stage.

'Hold up your right hand and be sworn,' the clerk said. 'Then give me your name and address.'

The woman complied.

'Miss Newton or Mrs Newton?'

'Mrs,' she said. 'I am a widow.'

'Very well, just take the stand.'

Dexter said, 'You live in the same apartment house as that in which the defendant lives?'

'I do.'

'Directing your attention to the thirteenth of this month, did you see the defendant at any time during the evening?'

'I did.'

'And where did you see the defendant?'

'She was going out of the door of her apartment – and I saw her all the way to the stairs.

'Now, I'd better explain that,' the witness went on glibly. 'You see, she lives on the third floor and she usually uses the elevator when she goes and comes. This time she didn't use the elevator. She was in such a hurry that—'

'Just a minute,' Dexter interrupted. 'It may be better if we cover this by question and answer, Mrs Newton. Now, can you give us the time that you saw the defendant?'

'Yes, sir, I can, exactly.'

'When was it?'

'Two minutes before eight o'clock in the evening.'

'And what was she doing when you saw her?'

'She was leaving her apartment. She walked rapidly from the apartment to the stair door.'

'Did she have anything in her hand?'

'She was carrying her canary.'

'You may cross-examine,' Dexter said.

Mason started his cross-examination with the caution that a veteran lawyer uses when it becomes apparent that the prosecution has dumped a witness in his lap knowing the defence attorney will have to cross-examine and that every answer the witness makes to questions on cross-examination is going to damn the defendant still more.

Mason said, 'How long have you lived in this apartment house, Mrs Newton?'

'Four years.'

'Do you know how long the defendant has lived there?'

'About eighteen months.'

'Are you inclined to be neighbourly?' Mason asked, smiling.

'Well, I mind my own business but I'm friendly.'

'Now, do you work?' Mason asked. 'Are you home all the time?'

'I don't work, and I'm not home all the time,' she said. 'I come and I go as I please. I have an income and don't have to work.'

'That's very fortunate,' Mason said. 'When did you first get acquainted with the defendant?'

'I saw her very shortly after she moved into the apartment.'

'That wasn't my question,' Mason said. 'I wanted to know when you first got acquainted with the defendant. When did you first talk with her?'

'Well, I don't know. I've said good morning and things like that. I guess I did that very shortly after she moved into the apartment.'

'I understand. But let me put it this way. When did you first start visiting with the defendant, talking with her?'

'Well, I don't know as I ever did talk with her much. She was a body who always kept pretty much to herself, and from what I'd heard around the apartment house—'

'Now, never mind what you've heard,' Mason said, 'and please try not to volunteer information, Mrs Newton. This hearing is being conducted according to strict rules of law and I want to ask you questions and have you answer just those questions and not volunteer any other information. Otherwise it might be necessary for me to ask the Court to strike out the parts of your answer that are not responsive.'

'Just don't volunteer any information,' Judge Madison said. 'Just listen to the question, then answer it. Do you understand?'

'Yes, Your Honour.'

Mason said, 'May I have the indulgence of the Court for just a moment, please?'

Mason turned to Maxine. 'What about her?' he whispered. 'Do you know her?'

'She's a gabby busybody,' Maxine said. 'She likes to visit with everybody in the apartment house and find out all about their affairs and then go blabber-mouth everything she finds out. She's lying. She lives on my floor, but I didn't go out at eight o'clock, and I didn't have any canary with me. I don't know what happened to my canary. I—'

'Never mind the details,' Mason said. 'I just wanted to get the picture. There's something funny here. Either the prosecutor wants me to lead with my chin and ask some question that will enable her to give a devastating answer, or there's a weak point in her testimony and he was trying to cover it up with a very terse direct examination.'

Dexter tilted back in his swivel chair at the counsel table, smiling across at Mason, knowing from long experience the predicament in which the lawyer found himself.

'That witness,' Mason said, 'is booby-trapped. I hardly dare open up any new gambit, and yet I *have* to cross-examine her.'

The lawyer looked up to see Judge Madison regarding him with a somewhat quizzical smile.

Mason returned to questioning the witness.

'Your apartment is on the same floor as that on which the defendant's apartment is located, Mrs Newton?'

'That's right.'

'And you were in your apartment at the time you saw the defendant?'

'I was not.'

'You were then perhaps walking down the corridor towards the elevator?'

'I was not.'

145

Mason hesitated a moment wondering whether he dared to quit or would have to go on and, catching a glimpse of Dexter's countenance, knew that he was walking into a trap.

'Were you,' Mason asked, 'standing still in the corridor, Mrs Newton?'

'I was standing still in the corridor,' she said. 'A friend of mine was coming up in the elevator and I was standing just outside the doorway of my apartment.'

'So your friend could find the apartment without difficulty?' Mason asked.

'Yes!'

'Was this friend a man or a woman?'

'Objected to as not proper cross-examination, incompetent, irrelevant, immaterial,' Dexter said.

'The objection is overruled,' Judge Madison said. 'The Court wasn't born yesterday, Mr Dexter, and the Court recognizes the technique you have used with your direct examination on this witness. I'll state one thing: The defence is going to have every latitude in the way of cross-examination. Proceed, Mr Mason, and the witness will answer the question.'

'It was a man,' Mrs Newton snapped.

'And this man had phoned that he was coming up in the elevator?'

'Yes.'

'And just how do you fix the time as being exactly two minutes off eight?' Mason asked.

Dexter's smile broadened into a grin.

'Because he was going to watch a certain television programme with me. He was late and I was afraid that the television programme would start before he arrived. So when he telephoned I looked at the clock and it was just a few minutes before eight o'clock, so I went to the apartment door and held it open for him.'

'Now let's get the location of your apartment,' Mason said. 'You're on the same floor as the apartment occupied by the defendant?'

'Yes, sir.'

'And you say that when the defendant left her apartment she went to the stairs instead of the elevator?'

'That's right.'

146

'And the stairs are located near the elevator?'

'They are not! They are located at the opposite end of the corridor.'

'And the defendant's apartment is between you and the elevator?'

'Between my apartment and the stairs,' she corrected.

'Oh, I see,' Mason said. 'Then you were standing in the corridor by the door of your apartment eagerly awaiting the visit of your boyfriend.'

'I didn't say he was my boyfriend, and I didn't have to be eager about it!' the witness snapped.

'Let me put it this way,' Mason said. 'You were anticipating the visit of a man who was coming to call on you; you were alone in your apartment at the time?'

'Yes.'

'He was going to watch a television programme with you?'

'Yes – among other things.'

'I see,' Mason repeated, with a slightly mocking smile, 'among other things, I believe you said?'

'That's what I *said*!'

'And you were waiting by the door of your apartment so that this friend of yours, this masculine friend, if you object to the term "boyfriend", Mrs Newton, wouldn't miss the apartment?'

'Well, I was showing him the apartment.'

'Then this was the first time he had been up there?' Mason said.

'I didn't say that.'

'Well, I'm asking you that. Was it the first time he had been up there?'

'No, it wasn't.'

Mason raised his eyebrows. 'Well, was the young man intoxicated, Mrs Newton?'

'Certainly not!'

'He was in full possession of his mental faculties, as far as you know?'

'Of course.'

'Then why was it necessary for you to stand at the door of your apartment in order to show him the location of the apartment, if he already knew where it was?'

'Well, I was being hospitable.'

'But that isn't what you said in your earlier testimony. You stated that you were standing there to show him the apartment.'

'Well, I was.'

'But he already knew the location of the apartment.'

'Well, I wanted to make certain he didn't forget.'

'How many times had he been to your apartment prior to this visit?'

'I don't know.'

'Oh, Your Honour,' Dexter said, 'this is getting entirely out of hand. This is becoming a cross-examination of this witness as to her social life and an attempt is being made to hold her to public ridicule simply because she was doing something that was perfectly natural: standing in the door of her apartment to welcome a visitor.'

'With open arms?' Mason asked.

Judge Madison smiled.

Dexter turned angrily to Mason and said, 'It was a thoroughly natural gesture, and you know it, and this examination is for the purpose of embarrassing the witness.'

'Not at all,' Mason said. 'I am simply trying to ascertain how it could be that if she was standing in the doorway watching the elevator for the purpose of seeing her friend as soon as he left the elevator in order to guide him to her apartment, she was also able to see behind her and notice the defendant leaving her apartment and walking in the opposite direction. I take it there is no claim she has eyes in the back of her head.'

Judge Madison said, 'Gentlemen, let's have no more personalities. Please address your remarks to the Court. This is quite plainly a case where a witness has been given a very perfunctory direct examination and counsel expects opposing counsel to develop the circumstances. Cross-examination of such a witness is, well, to use a popular expression, it's loaded with dynamite. The defence attorney is forced to cross-examine, and he's proceeding in the dark, realizing, of course, the danger which exists.

'The Court is watching the development of the situation with a great deal of interest, just as the prosecutor is watching it with a great deal of amusement. The Court certainly doesn't intend to interfere as long as the cross-examination is within anything like reasonable limits, and the Court will confess that it has been puzzled as to how the witness could see the defendant emerge from her apartment, which was opposite to the direction in which the witness was looking, and follow her all the way to the stairs, while at the same time she was watching the elevator.'

'Well,' Mrs Newton snapped, 'I didn't have to *stare* at the elevator. I was conscious of other things that were taking place. I didn't keep my eyes riveted on the elevator.'

'Don't argue with me,' Judge Madison said to the witness, 'and don't volunteer information. Mr Mason will doubtless cover this point by questioning, and you may answer his questions.'

The grin had faded from Dexter's face. He now seemed slightly concerned.

Mason said, 'Now you have fixed the time as being two minutes off eight, Mrs Newton?'

'I have.'

'And you approximated that time because of—'

'I didn't approximate it. That's accurate.'

'And just how did you fix it?'

'Because the television programme we wanted to watch came on at eight o'clock.'

'You had expected this boyfriend of yours earlier?'

'I didn't say he was my boyfriend.'

'He was a man?'

'Yes.'

'He was a friend?'

'Naturally.'

'Then I'll refer to him as a man friend,' Mason said. 'You had expected this man friend earlier?'

'I'd been waiting for him ever since ... well, half past seven.'

'That was when he was due to arrive?'

'That was when I expected him.'

'So you were annoyed at the delay?'

'I was somewhat apprehensive.'

'Apprehensive?' Mason asked. 'You thought perhaps he wasn't coming?'

'No, I thought perhaps something had happened to him.'

'He'd been up to your apartment before?'

'I already said he had.'

'Was he in the habit of coming late?'

'I don't make appointments by the clock.'

'But this time you did?'

'I made this appointment by the television.'

'Did you make the appointment, or did he?'

'Well, I suggested that ... well, I don't know. It's just one of those things that happen.'

'So you were a little apprehensive as you were watching the elevator?'

'I had been apprehensive prior to that time. I wasn't apprehensive when I was watching the elevator; I was expectant.'

'Was the defendant standing in the hall when you opened the door?'

'No, she came out afterwards.'

'You saw her when she emerged?'

'Well, I ... yes.'

'Did you see her when she was emerging?' Mason asked.

'What do you mean by that?'

'Did you see her as soon as she opened the door?'

'The door was opened once and then closed again, and then opened the second time and the defendant came out holding this canary-cage. She closed the door and hurried down the corridor.'

'Did you speak to her?'

'I didn't have the chance.'

'What do you mean?'

'She didn't even turn around.'

'Oh, then her back was to you?' Mason said.

'Naturally. If she was going to the stairway, her back had to be towards me. She wouldn't have walked backwards.'

There was a slight titter in the courtroom. Judge Madison started to say something, then smiled and settled back in his chair.

'Did she have her back to you when she came out the door?' Mason asked.

'Yes.'

'Did you take your eyes off the elevator while you were watching her?'

'No, I— Well, I was sort of looking in both directions.'

'At the same time?'

'Well, alternating.'

'You were turning your head back and forth just as rapidly as you could turn it?'

'Certainly not! I was primarily interested in the elevator. I saw the defendant – well, just like you'd see anything incidentally.'

'And was her back to you when she came out of the apartment carrying the bird-cage?'

'Yes. She backed out of the apartment, holding the bird-cage.'

'Pulled the door shut and walked rapidly towards the stairs?'

'I've already told you that a dozen times.'

'So you never did see her face,' Mason said.

'I didn't have to see her face to recognize her. I recognized her figure; I recognized her clothing.'

'So you didn't see her face?'

'I saw her clothes.'

'So you didn't see her face?'

'No.'

'What was she wearing?'

'A tweed coat.'

'Can you describe that coat? Was it tight-fitting or—'

'No, it was a loose-fitting, baggy, tweed coat.'

'A long coat or a short coat?'

'A long coat. It came to her knees – a little below.'

'You'd seen her in that coat before?'

'Many times.'

'And during all this time you were waiting for your man friend to emerge from the elevator?'

'Yes.'

'And keeping your eye on the elevator so that he wouldn't miss your apartment?'

'I wanted to welcome him.'

'Then you were standing there not because you wanted him to know where the apartment was, but because you wanted to give him your welcome in person?'

'Oh, if the Court please,' Dexter said, 'that question has been answered several times.'

'And in several different ways,' Judge Madison said. 'The witness may answer the question.'

'All right!' she said angrily. 'I don't know why I was standing there. It was just a natural gesture. I was ... well, I was there, and it doesn't make any difference *why* I was there. I was there and I saw this defendant emerge from her apartment carrying that caged canary.'

'When your man friend emerged from the elevator, did you run towards him?'

'No.'

'Did you walk towards him?'

'No.'

'You just stood there and let him walk all the way?'

'Well, I moved a few steps.'

'Walking, or running?'

'Walking.'

'Then you did walk to meet him?'

'Well, not all the way.'

'Part of the way?'

'Yes.'

'And during that time you had your back turned to the defendant?'

'She had gone before that. She opened the stair door and just shot through it.'

'Before your man friend emerged from the elevator?'

'At just about the same time.'

'What were the lighting conditions in the hallway of the apartment house, Mrs Newton? The lighting was rather dim, I take it?'

'Well, you take it wrong,' she said. 'I had been complaining about the lighting and so had some of the other tenants and beginning with the first of the year the management had put in a whole new series of lights – and it was high time they did it. The way things had been it was just as dark as a pocket. A body could have got herself hurt there.'

'So the lighting conditions were good?'

'They were.'

Mason hesitated a moment. 'Do you have a driving licence, Mrs Newton?'

'Of course I do.'

'May I see it?'

'Well, I certainly don't see what that has to do with it,' the witness said.

'Nor do I,' Dexter announced, getting to his feet. 'If the Court please, I think it is incompetent, irrelevant, and immaterial.'

Judge Madison shook his head. 'This is cross-examination,' he said. 'This witness has testified to a recognition of the defendant under circumstances which could be very vital to the defence, and I have no intention of limiting the cross-examination of defence counsel as long as the examination is within reasonable limits. Moreover, the Court thinks it knows what counsel is after and it is certainly pertinent.'

The witness reluctantly opened her purse, produced her driving licence. 'This gives the date of my birth,' she said, 'and I certainly don't want to have my age published in the newspapers. I just don't think it's anyone's business.'

'I wasn't interested in the date of your birth,' Mason said, taking the driving licence. 'I was interested in whether there were any restrictions – ah yes, I see that your driving licence says that you must wear corrective glasses.'

'Well, what about it?' snapped the witness.

'You don't seem to have any glasses on now.'

'Well, I'm not driving a car now.'

'And you weren't driving a car on the night of the thirteenth when you saw a figure that you thought you could recognize as that of the defendant.'

'I didn't see a figure I thought I could recognize as that of the defendant. I saw the defendant. She was walking out of that apartment carrying her bird-cage, and I just said to myself, I said to myself—'

'Never mind what you said to yourself,' Mason interrupted with a smile, 'that would be hearsay. Let me ask you, Mrs Newton, can you see the headline on this newspaper I'm holding up?'

'Certainly I can see it. And I can read it. And I can read the smaller headlines. I can read those headlines over in the right-'

hand corner: PRESIDENT CONTEMPLATES BALANCED BUDGET FOR NEXT FISCAL YEAR.'

Mason frowned thoughtfully, said abruptly, 'Are you wearing contact lenses, Mrs Newton?'

'Yes!'

'When did you first wear contact lenses?'

'I got them on the afternoon of the twelfth.'

'And discarded your other glasses?'

'Not all at once. I alternated – I still do.'

'So on the thirteenth you hadn't as yet become fully accustomed to your contact lenses?'

'Well, I could see with them all right.'

'But you were wearing them only a short time each day?'

'Yes.'

'Did you have them on when you emerged from your apartment and saw the figure you take to be that of the defendant in the corridor?'

'I don't remember.'

'Well, let's see if we can refresh your memory,' Mason said. 'When did you put them in on the thirteenth, in the morning?'

'I don't remember.'

'You recognized the figure you now say was that of the defendant, by the clothes?'

'I'd know that tweed coat of hers anywhere.'

'It wasn't form-fitting?'

'I've told you it wasn't. It was a baggy, tweed coat.'

Mason said, 'Then you couldn't see the face, you couldn't see the figure. All you could see was the coat and the caged canary.'

'What more do you want?'

'*I* don't want anything,' Mason said, smiling, 'except to have you tell the truth. Now, you couldn't recognize the defendant by her form, could you, because you couldn't see her form.'

'That question is argumentative, if the Court please,' Dexter said.

'I'm going to allow it anyway,' Judge Madison said. 'I think the situation is quite obvious here and if counsel wants to develop it for the record I'm going to permit him to do so.'

'I couldn't see her figure; she had her clothes on.'

'By clothes you mean this baggy, tweed coat?'

'She had other clothes on.'

'But you couldn't see them.'

'I can't see through a coat. I don't have X-ray eyes.'

'So all you could see was a figure wearing a tweed coat.'

'Well, I guess I know the coat when I see it.'

'And carrying a bird in a cage.'

'A caged canary.'

'Could you see the bird?'

'I saw the bird well enough to know it was a canary.'

'And in view of the fact that you didn't intend to drive your car,' Mason said, 'the probabilities are that you didn't have your glasses on. Is that correct?'

'All right,' the witness snapped, 'I *didn't* have my glasses on, but I'm not blind, Mr Mason.'

'Thank you,' Mason said. 'That's all!'

'No redirect,' Dexter said.

'Call your next witness,' Judge Madison directed.

'That's our case, Your Honour,' Dexter said. 'The People rest.'

'Well,' Judge Madison said, 'of course the testimony has some gaps, as Mr Mason has so dramatically pointed out. The defendant was seen near this locker. However, she was not seen opening the locker, or putting anything in it.

'Of course, however, it is her gun and, while Mr Mason's dramatic cross-examination of the last witness indicates that there may be weak links in the evidence, there seems to be no alternative for this Court but to bind the defendant over and...'

Mason rose.

'And since it is a murder case,' Judge Madison went on, 'the defendant will not be admitted to bail.'

'May I make a statement, if the Court please?' Mason asked.

'Certainly,' Judge Madison said.

'The defendant wishes to put on a case.'

Judge Madison frowned, hesitated a moment, then spoke cautiously, weighing his words. 'The Court had no intention of precluding the defendant from putting on a case. The Court had naturally assumed that there would be no defence, since this is merely a preliminary hearing.

'The Court apologizes to counsel for starting to make its order binding the defendant over without asking the defendant's counsel if he wished to put on any case.

'Having said that, however, may the Court point out that in a matter of this sort where the only question before the Court is whether a crime has been committed and there is reasonable ground to believe the defendant committed that crime, it does no good to raise a conflict in the evidence. The Court's duty is apparent.

'I take it the defence understands this somewhat elemental situation?'

'The defence understands it,' Mason said.

'Very well,' Judge Madison said, 'if you wish to put on a defence, go ahead.'

Mason said, 'I'll call Goring Gilbert to the stand.'

Gilbert, his shirt now buttoned and tucked in his slacks, and wearing shoes and a sports coat, came forward, raised his right hand and seated himself on the witness-stand.

After the witness had given his name and address to the clerk of the court, Mason said abruptly, 'Did you know Collin Max Durant in his lifetime?'

'I did.'

'Did you have any business transactions with him?'

'Several.'

'Within the last several weeks did you have any business transactions?'

'Yes.'

'As a result of that business, did he give you a sum of money?'

'Yes. He paid me for some of the work I did.'

'How was that money paid to you, in cash or by cheque?'

'In cash.'

'And how was it paid in cash? Were there bills of any particular denomination?'

'The last money I received from him was all in one-hundred-dollar bills.'

Judge Madison frowned thoughtfully and leaned forward on the bench to look down at the witness.

'And what were you hired to do?' Mason asked.

'I was hired to do various paintings.'

'You completed those paintings?'

'I did.'

'And what did you do with them?'

'They were delivered to Collin Durant.'

'Do you know where those paintings are now?'

'No.'

'What?' Mason exclaimed.

'I said I didn't know where they were.'

'I will call your attention to a painting I examined at your studio, one that was in the style of a painter named—'

'I am familiar with *that* painting.'

'Where is it now?'

'I have it.'

'You were served with a *subpoena duces tecum* to bring a painting with you?'

'I was.'

'That was the same painting I looked at in your studio?'

'Yes.'

'And you have the painting here?'

'Yes. It is wrapped up and in the witness-room.'

'Will you get it, please?'

'Now, just a moment,' Dexter said. 'I haven't objected to the line of examination, if the Court please, because I felt certain counsel intended to connect it up.

'As far as the one-hundred-dollar bills are concerned, it is possible – *barely* possible – that the testimony is pertinent. But as far as *this* painting is concerned, it is very plainly incompetent, irrelevant, and immaterial, and I object to it on that ground.'

'So it would seem,' Judge Madison ruled. 'The payment in one-hundred-dollar bills is an interesting development, but unless those one-hundred-dollar bills can be identified in some manner – I take it counsel intends to connect them up?'

Judge Madison looked at Perry Mason. Mason said, 'If the Court please, I intend to connect up *this* painting.'

Judge Madison shook his head. 'I don't see that the painting can be at all relevant. The money that was paid for the painting might have some bearing.'

Mason said, 'I intend to connect up the painting, Your Honour.'

'No,' Judge Madison said, 'I think you should go at it the other way, Counsellor. I think you should first show the fact that the painting is pertinent according to some phase of the case before you try to introduce it.'

'I intend to do that,' Mason said.

'I think you had better do it, then.'

'However,' Mason said, 'while this witness is here, if the Court rules that I can't have this painting introduced in evidence, I certainly would like to have it marked for identification and retained in the custody of the clerk until I have connected it up.'

'I take it there is no objection to that procedure?' Judge Madison asked Dexter.

Dexter seemed somewhat uncertain. After a moment he got to his feet. 'If the Court please, this witness is here in response to a *subpoena duces tecum*, he has brought the painting, the painting isn't going to run away.'

'Paintings don't run away,' Mason said, 'but it might be taken away.'

'Well, it's here now. It can be brought back at a later date.'

'If it is marked for identification and left in the custody of the Court, it will—'

'Very well,' Judge Madison interrupted. 'The Court is going to so rule. Produce the painting, Counsellor.'

Mason said to Gilbert, 'Will you produce the painting, please?'

Gilbert, sullen, plainly hostile, hesitated. 'It's my painting. I don't think that anyone has any right to take it away from me.'

'Produce it, please, and we'll take a look at it,' Judge Madison said. 'That is the Court's ruling.'

Gilbert left the witness-stand, went to the ante-room, shortly returned with a painting covered with wrapping paper. He angrily ripped off the wrapping paper and held up the painting.

Judge Madison looked at the painting, blinked his eyes, and looked again at Gilbert. 'Did you do that, young man?' he asked.

'Yes, Your Honour.'

'That's a *very* good painting,' Judge Madison said.

'Thank you.'

'You may resume your position on the witness-stand.'

Gilbert walked back to the witness-stand.

'This painting that you have produced,' Mason asked, 'is one that you did at the request of Collin M. Durant, the decedent?'

'Now, just a moment, before you answer that question,' Dexter said, 'I'm going to object to this on the ground that it is incompetent, irrelevant, and immaterial; that this painting has absolutely no bearing on the issues in the case.'

'At the present time I think that is correct. The objection will be sustained.'

'I ask, if the Court please, that this painting be marked for identification,' Mason said.

'So ordered,' Judge Madison said.

'And left with the clerk in the custody of the Court.'

'For how long?' Judge Madison asked. 'How long do you think it will take you to get to the matter in hand, Counsellor?'

'I would like to have until tomorrow to do so.'

'You mean you have a case which is going to take all afternoon?' the judge inquired.

'If the Court please,' Mason said, 'I intend to put the defendant on the stand.'

'Put the defendant on the stand!' Judge Madison echoed incredulously.

'Yes, Your Honour.'

Dexter jumped up, paused openmouthed, looked at Mason, looked at the judge, and then slowly sat down.

'And,' Mason said, 'in order to prepare for this rather unexpected development in the case, I would like to have a recess until three-thirty this afternoon. I may state to the Court that my determination to put on a defence was not reached until a few minutes before the prosecution concluded its case.'

'You have a right to put on a defence and you have a right to have a reasonable continuance in order to get your witnesses here,' Judge Madison said. 'Do I understand, Mr Mason, that you now state you are going to put the defendant on the witness-stand?'

159

'I am going to put the defendant on the witness-stand,' Mason said.

'Very well, that's your privilege,' Judge Madison said. 'I may point out that it is very seldom, if ever, done in a preliminary hearing in a murder case.'

'Yes, Your Honour.'

Judge Madison said, 'I suppose you know what you're doing. . . . Very well. Court will take a recess until three-thirty. . . . I would like to see counsel for the defendant in chambers, please.'

'Yes, Your Honour,' Mason said.

Judge Madison left the bench and went into his chambers. Dexter said to Mason, 'What kind of a stunt are you trying to pull now?'

'No stunt at all,' Mason said. 'The defendant certainly has a right to let the Court know her story.'

'You mean to let the newspapers know it.'

'Any way you want it,' Mason said.

'It's your party,' Dexter said, 'and it's your funeral.' He picked up his briefcase and walked out.

Mason went into chambers, and Judge Madison, hanging up his robe in the closet, turned to the lawyer and said, 'Now, look here, Mason. I've known you for a long time. You're a shrewd, clever lawyer. You have a good-looking client who is very probably going to appeal to the sympathies of a jury, but you know this Court well enough to know that tears and nylon are not going to have an effect on my judgement.'

'Yes, Judge,' Mason said.

'All right. Don't do it.'

'Don't do what?'

'Don't put your defendant on the stand. You know better than that. You get her on the witness-stand and there'll be a record made of her testimony, they'll try to tear her to pieces with cross-examination, and then when she gets in the Superior Court she has two strikes against her. Everything she says, every answer she gives, has got to be exactly like the story she told at the preliminary hearing. Now, I'd feel different about it if it could do any good, but I just want to tell you off the record what I told you on the record in court. I'm going to bind this defendant over for trial and no amount of explaining or denial on her part is going to stop me.

'It was her gun that killed Durant. He was killed in her apartment. She resorted to flight immediately after the murder. She left the apartment without even pausing long enough to pack up her things. All she took with her was her canary. She lied to the officers about the time she left the apartment and she went down to the bus station and stayed down there until she could get you on the phone. She concealed the gun in one of the lockers there and left it. Then she gave your secretary the key to her apartment and skipped out.

'Now, you may be able to beat that case in front of a jury. You're clever and you have a good-looking client. But you can't figure out any possible combination of facts which would keep a committing magistrate from binding the defendant over under circumstances such as that, so why lead with your chin?'

Mason said, 'I'm taking a calculated risk.'

Judge Madison said, 'The minute I make an order binding that defendant over for trial, every lawyer in the country is going to be grinning and stopping his brother lawyers and saying: "Did you hear about Perry Mason's goof?"'

'I know it,' Mason said.

'Damn it!' Judge Madison expostulated. 'I'm your friend. I'm trying to keep you from doing something you'll regret.'

'I'm going to take a calculated risk,' Mason said.

'All right,' Madison said, 'go ahead and take it. But just remember that tears and nylon mean nothing to me.'

'I'll remember,' Mason said.

CHAPTER SEVENTEEN

Mason, in the detention room off the courtroom, smiled reassuringly at Maxine Lindsay as a policewoman brought her in.

'Maxine,' Mason said, 'I'm going to do something that is ordinarily considered a great mistake. I'm going to put you on the stand in a preliminary hearing and let you tell your story.'

'I want to tell it.'

'They're going to cross-examine you. They're going to rip you up the back and down the front.'

'I expect that.'

'They're going to cast slurs and innuendos and they're going on a fishing expedition.'

'What do you mean by a fishing expedition?'

'They'll ask you all sorts of questions, hoping that you'll lie about something. They'll ask you about your past, about—'

'You mean they'll inquire into my—'

'They'll be circumspect,' Mason interrupted, 'but they'll ask you how long you lived in a certain place, at what address you lived; they'll ask you if you were going under your own name or another name. In other words, they'll try to explore. If you were living with some man as his wife—'

'I wasn't.'

'I'm just warning you,' Mason said. 'Now, I'm going to try to short-cut their cross-examination. I'm going to put you on the stand, let you tell a part of your story, then ask to withdraw you temporarily. I don't know whether I can get away with that or not.'

'But won't that just be postponing things?'

'It will be postponing them,' Mason said, 'but it just *may* postpone them long enough so we can mix up the whole case. The way things stand in this case at present, you don't stand a ghost of a show. The judge is going to bind you over for trial. That means you'll be held without bail on a charge of first-degree murder. I don't want that to happen. You don't want that to happen.'

'Well,' she said, 'I could take a little of it but I ... I certainly don't want to get convicted by a jury – particularly for something I didn't do.'

'I know,' Mason said, 'and I'm taking chances. But it's a gamble I think we should take. I'm putting it right up to you, Maxine, if you don't want—'

'I want you to do what you think is best, Mr Mason.'

'I want to put you on the stand,' Mason said, 'just long enough to get that false Feteet introduced in evidence. I think I can do it if I have your testimony. Now remember, Maxine, you're twenty-nine. You're a mature woman. Under present conditions people hardly expect that you are— Well, if you have ever lived with anyone as his wife, go ahead and say so when they ask you if you've ever used any other names. You can call it a common-law marriage. Just don't let them catch you in a lie. No matter what you do, tell the truth, because they'll have weeks to investigate every statement you make and if they can get you up in front of a jury and make you admit that you lied under oath, your chances of escaping conviction are very slim indeed.'

'I understand,' she said.

'All right,' Mason told her. 'Here we go – and if you've been lying to me, heaven help you.'

Mason returned to rejoin Della Street.

Della Street, looking at shorthand notes, said, 'Chief, did you get the significance of Gilbert's answer to the question about the painting? I gathered from what he said that this was *not* one of the paintings that Durant had had him do.'

'I got it,' Mason said, 'and I don't know what it means. I've gone so far now that I can't back up. I've got to keep moving. I think he *may* have misunderstood the question. However, I don't dare to back up now.

'It may be that Durant didn't deal with him directly on this, but was going to buy it after Gilbert had made the copy but— Didn't he tell us that Durant had him paint it when we were at his studio? No, wait a minute, I guess he didn't say so in so many words.'

'I gathered he did,' Della Street said.

'No,' Mason said, frowning thoughtfully. 'I asked him if he'd done paintings for Durant and he said he had. I asked him if they were forgeries and he said they weren't forgeries in that sense of the word; that Durant sold them as conversation pieces which could be bought for peanuts. Then I asked him if he hadn't done a painting of women under a tree in the style of Phellipe Feteet, and he hesitated a minute and then went over to the pile of paintings and pulled this one out and asked me if that answered my question.'

'Well?' Della Street asked.

Mason said, 'There's something very strange here. I'm going to try and get that picture in evidence. Once I get it in evidence I'm going to make scrambled eggs out of the district attorney's case; at least I'm going to try to.'

'And Paul Drake is busy serving subpoenas?'

'Paul Drake is busy with subpoenas,' Mason said, 'and the first thing you know all hell is going to break loose. Olney is going to be calling the judge and saying he doesn't want to be a witness, and that he doesn't know anything about the case, and he'll have his lawyers bustling into court claiming that I've abused the process of the court, and, by the time we get done, we'll have a three-ring circus around here.'

'And what will the judge do?' Della Street asked.

Mason said, 'Unless I can pull a great big, fat, kicking rabbit out of the hat, the judge is going to bind Maxine over, but I can't back up now. If I did, everyone would think that I found out Maxine was guilty during the recess, that she confessed to me or something, and I didn't dare to go ahead. That would be highly detrimental to her when the case comes on for trial in front of a jury. I'm just going to tear in and thrust and slash and kick up such a hell of a commotion nobody will know who is accusing whom of what.'

'And what will the prosecution be doing all of that time?'

'The prosecution,' Mason said, 'will be almost certain to have our esteemed contemporary, Hamilton Burger, the district attorney, attending the balance of the trial in person so that he can enjoy my discomfiture when I put the defendant on the stand and throw my case out the window.

'Hamilton Burger will be the one to take the credit for forcing me to commit a legal error.'

'He's clever,' Della Street warned.

'I know he's clever,' Mason said, 'but I jumped in my boat and pushed it out into the middle of the stream. I'm just above the rapids now. I've either got to shoot them, or capsize. I can't turn around and go back, and if I should try to, it would be much worse than being capsized once I got in the rapids. The only thing to do now is to keep on paddling downstream, pretending to be confident that I know a channel among the rocks.'

CHAPTER EIGHTEEN

Hamilton Burger, the district attorney, was personally present when court reconvened. He was seated beside his trial deputy, his manner indicating very plainly that he felt Perry Mason had blundered, and the district attorney, who had long been feuding with the defence lawyer, intending to be there in person to take full advantage of the opening Mason had given.

'I call Maxine Lindsay to the stand,' Mason said. 'Just go up there and hold up your right hand, Maxine. And,' he added, 'tell the truth.'

'No need of the grandstand,' Hamilton Burger said. 'There's no jury here.'

Judge Madison smiled but said quietly, 'I would like to have counsel refrain from personalities, please.'

Mason said, 'Maxine, you remember the night of the thirteenth?'

'Very well,' she said.

'You knew Collin Durant in his lifetime?'

'Yes.'

'How long had you known him?'

'Some— I can't remember. Three or four years.'

'Were you friendly with him?'

'I hd been friendly with him and – well, I knew him. I did things for him.'

'Now,' Mason said, 'I want you to listen to my questions very carefully, Maxine, and answer the questions without volunteering information.'

'Yes, sir.'

'Are you acquainted with Otto Olney?'

'I am.'

'Were you present on his yacht at a time when you had a conversation with Mr Durant about one of Mr Olney's paintings?'

'Yes.'

'And what did Mr Durant say?'

Judge Madison pursed his lips. 'We're now getting into a realm where—'

Hamilton Burger jumped to his feet. 'If the Court please,' he said, 'we are not making any objection. We want Mr Mason to go right ahead. Every subject that he opens up gives us a new gambit for cross-examination. We don't intend to object to any question he may ask.'

'I can appreciate the attitude of the district attorney,' Judge Madison said, 'but after all, this Court has a crowded calendar. . . . However, there being no objection. I'll let the question stand.'

'Can you tell us what happened with reference to one of the paintings?' Mason asked.

'Mr Durant came to me and told me that a painting Mr Olney had on his yacht, a painting supposedly by Phellipe Feteet, was a fake. Later on he told me to report that conversation to Mr Rankin.'

'And who is Mr Rankin?'

'That is Lattimer Rankin, an art dealer. He was, I believe, the art dealer who had sold Mr Olney the picture.'

'And what did Mr Durant tell you about this picture?'

'He said in effect that I was to tell Mr Rankin that he, Durant, had pronounced the picture a fake and that it was a fraud.'

'That was a painting of some women under a tree?'

'Yes.'

Mason said, 'I am going to show you a picture which was marked for identification and ask you if that is the same picture.'

Judge Madison looked at Hamilton Burger. 'No objection,' Hamilton Burger said, beaming. 'We want counsel to have all the rope he wants to take.'

Judge Madison pointed out, 'This probably will lay the foundation for the introduction of that picture in evidence.'

'If he wants to put the defendant on the stand in order to get it in, let him put it in,' Hamilton Burger said. 'Let him put in anything he wants, let him open all doors for our cross-examination.'

'Very well,' Judge Madison said crisply.

Mason said, 'I'll put it this way, Maxine. I'm going to show you a picture which was marked for identification. You saw that picture at the time it was brought into court?'

'I did.'

'Now, listen to the question carefully, Maxine. Is that picture, the painting which I now show you and which has been marked tentatively for identification as Defendant's Exhibit Number One, is that the painting, the one Mr Durant pointed out to you, and which he told you to tell Mr Rankin was a forgery?'

'I don't know.'

'Can you answer the question any better than that?'

'I'll say this, it is a painting that is absolutely similar. If it isn't the same one that was hanging there, it looks like the same one.'

'Now, on the night of the thirteenth did you have any further conversation with Mr Durant?'

'I did.'

'At what time?'

'At about six o'clock in the evening.'

'And what did Mr Durant tell you at that time?'

'Mr Durant told me to get out of town, fast, and not to leave any trail – not to stop to take anything with me, just to get out.'

'When did he tell you to leave?'

'Within an hour. He said I couldn't be in my apartment any later than that.'

'Did you have any conversation about money?'

'I told him that I didn't have enough money to travel and he said that he would try to get me some money. He said I was to wait an hour for him to return, that if he could raise some money for me he would do so; that if he couldn't, I would have to get along as best I could, even if I had to hitch-hike or wire my sister for money.'

'You have a married sister living in Eugene, Oregon?'

'I do.'

'Did you report to Mr Durant that you had told Mr Rankin that the picture in Otto Olney's yacht, in the main saloon of that yacht, the picture purporting to be by Phellipe Feteet, was a fake?'

'Yes.'

'And did you tell him anything you had done in connection with that litigation?'

'Yes. I told him that I had signed an affidavit in your office, stating that Mr Durant had told me the Phellipe Feteet in Otto Olney's yacht was a fake.'

'And it was after you had made that statement to Mr Durant that he told you to get out of town?'

'Yes.'

'Now I'm going to ask you, Maxine, if Mr Durant had some hold on you?'

'He did, yes.'

'There was some bit of information that he was threatening to disclose if you did not do as he wished?'

'Yes.'

Mason said, 'If the Court please, I feel that this painting should now be introduced in evidence.'

'We object to having the painting introduced in evidence at this time,' Hamilton Burger said. 'There is nothing to show that it is a forged Phellipe Feteet painting, there is nothing to show that it ever hung on the wall of the main saloon in Otto Olney's yacht and—'

'We don't claim that it ever hung on the wall there,' Mason said. 'We don't think it did.'

'What?' Judge Madison asked, puzzled.

'I think, if the Court please,' Mason said, 'the plot was much deeper than appeared on the surface.'

Hamilton Burger said, 'Of course, if the Court please, this whole thing is extraneous except as it shows motivation for murder, and we want to develop that gambit on cross-examination. However, let us suppose that the decedent was a swindler who was engaged in an attempt to swindle Mr Olney or Mr Rankin or both; that still doesn't give the defendant the licence to murder him. We don't have an open season on swindlers, nor do we have an open season on blackmailers.'

Judge Madison said, 'The fact remains, Mr Mason, that this painting which has been marked for identification is so far an isolated issue in the case. In other words, a witness has testified that the decedent paid him to make several paintings. But that witness said, unless I misunderstood him, that this painting was one he had been hired to make but he didn't state specifically it was Durant who had employed him to make it. *Now* the defendant has testified that this painting looks like one that was hanging in the main saloon of a yacht, and which Durant told her was a forgery. But we haven't established that it is either a copy, or a forgery, or the original.'

'Exactly,' Mason said, 'and I want to be able to establish exactly what it is.'

'Well, go ahead and establish it,' Judge Madison said. 'For all the present testimony shows, this could be the original. It looks too good to be a copy.'

'In order to establish what it is,' Mason said, frowning thoughtfully, and apparently conceding the point reluctantly, 'I would have to withdraw this witness temporarily and ask some more questions of the previous witness, Goring Gilbert.'

'Very well,' Judge Madison said, 'if you want to get that painting in evidence at this time we will have a *voir dire* examination in regard to the painting. You may step down, Miss Lindsay, and Mr Gilbert will take the stand.'

Hamilton Burger half got to his feet as though to object, then hesitated and dropped back into his chair.

Mason, biting his lip, apparently with annoyance, turned so that his back was to Hamilton Burger and gave Della Street a reassuring wink.

Gilbert once more took the stand.

'Were you hired to make a copy of a painting that was in the yacht of Otto Olney?'

Gilbert said, 'Yes.'

'And you made such a copy?'

'Yes.'

'And this painting which I now show you, which is marked for identification as Defendant's Exhibit Number One, was that painting?'

'Yes.'

'You were paid for it?'

'Yes.'

'How much?'

'Two thousand dollars.'

'How were you paid?'

'Haven't we gone all over this?' Judge Madison asked.

'This is now preliminary merely and I want to be sure the

foundation is in,' Mason said, glancing surreptitiously at the clock.

'Very well, very well,' Judge Madison said. 'Go ahead.'

'I was paid two thousand dollars in cash, in the form of twenty one-hundred-dollar bills.'

'And you made this copy?'

'I did.'

'I think that's all the questions I have of this witness,' Mason said. 'I take it the prosecutor has no desire to cross-examine this witness.'

'On the contrary,' Hamilton Burger said, 'the prosecution certainly does intend to cross-examine this witness. And while the prosecution intends to give the defence counsel every latitude in asking questions of the defendant, the prosecution intends to object to the introduction of this painting at this time. It hasn't been connected up with anything.'

'This is on *voire dire* to identify the painting,' Judge Madison said. 'It is a limited proceeding, simply for the purpose of laying a foundation.'

'That's why I want to cross-examine the witness.'

'Very well, go ahead,' Judge Madison ordered. 'We still have a few minutes before adjournment.'

'I doubt if I can complete my cross-examination before time for adjournment.'

'It's all right. Go ahead and start your questions.'

'When did you first talk with Durant about copying pictures?' Hamilton Burger asked.

'About a year ago.'

'And you made copies of several pictures for him?'

'Not exact copies. I copied the *style*, not the picture.'

'But this picture is an exact copy?'

'Yes.'

'Of a painting owned by Otto Olney?'

'Yes.'

'And Durant paid you to make this copy?'

'No.'

'What?'

'I said no.'

'Oh, I see. He didn't pay you, so you retained possession of the picture, is that right?'

'No.'

'Didn't you say you were paid two thousand dollars in hundred-dollar bills for making this picture?'

'Yes.'

'And then you retained the picture?'

'Yes.'

Burger, suddenly suspicious of a trap, hesitated, then bent over for a whispered conference with Dexter.

After a few seconds he straightened and said, 'Did the defendant pay you to make this copy?'

'No.'

'Who did?'

'It has no connection with this case, so I am not going to divulge the name of my client.'

'Whether it has any connection with this case isn't for you to say, young man,' Hamilton Burger thundered. 'I want an answer to my question.'

'Just a moment,' Mason said. 'The district attorney is not entitled to an answer to that question unless he concedes that the painting is pertinent to the case. If the painting is entirely without the issues of this case, then the district attorney isn't entitled to an answer to that question.'

'You've made it a part of the case,' Hamilton Burger said. 'I have a right to cross-examine the witness on anything you've brought out on direct examination.'

Mason said, 'I didn't bring out the name of the person who had hired him to make the painting.'

'I understood it was Collin Durant,' Burger said.

'Go back and look at the testimony,' Mason said, 'and you'll see the witness never said it was Collin Durant.'

'Well, I'm entitled to an answer to my question.'

Mason said, 'If the Court please, the prosecution can't eat its cake and have it too. If the prosecution wants to stipulate that this painting is a part of this case and that it is a material factor in the case, then I am entitled to have the painting introduced in evidence and the prosecutor can force the witness to answer this question, unless, of course' – here Mason paused and glanced significantly at the witness, slowing his diction so the words came slowly and distinctly – 'unless, I repeat, he should state *that the answer to that question would*

171

involve him in a crime, in which event the witness couldn't be forced to answer the question.'

Judge Madison regarded Burger's flushed face, then looked at Mason, then at the defendant. 'This is a most peculiar situation,' he said.

'I'm entitled to cross-examine any witness that the defendant puts on the stand as to any matter connected with the testimony the witness has given,' Hamilton Burger said doggedly.

'But this is a proceeding in *voir dire*,' Judge Madison ruled.

'That makes no difference. I'm entitled to a cross-examination.'

'Provided the question relates to issues which are relevant to the case. You can't cross-examine a witness on issues which are irrelevant, despite the fact that the witness may have been asked those questions on direct examination.

'Now, you will remember, Mr District Attorney, that the Court called your attention to the fact that some of the questions called for irrelevant testimony, but you stated that you weren't going to make any objection, that you wanted the defence to open up all possible doors for your cross-examination.

'*You* may adopt that attitude, but it is not binding on the Court. The Court doesn't have to sit here and listen to a lot of evidence which is entirely extraneous. Now, the Court is inclined to believe that Mr Mason is correct; that if you are going to insist on an answer to something which was not brought out in direct examination and which is not relevant, then the defence is entitled to object. The only way that it would be relevant for you to inquire into the antecedents of this picture would be if the picture itself is going to be introduced in evidence.'

'Well, the defence is trying to get it introduced,' Burger said.

'And you're trying to keep it out,' Judge Madison ruled. 'Now I want to give everyone every opportunity to present competent evidence, but I don't want to have time taken up with extraneous matters.

'I noticed earlier in the day that this witness did not definitely state that Collin Durant had commissioned him to paint this particular picture, and now he has gone further and has

172

stated definitely that Collin Durant did not hire him to make this copy. Now then, you want to know who did. That question certainly is of no relevance unless it has some bearing on the case itself, and it can have no bearing on the case unless the picture is to become a part of the case.'

'Well, I want to know about it,' Hamilton Burger said, 'and I think I'm entitled to.'

'Do you now concede then, that the picture is a part of the defendant's case?'

'No, I do not.'

'At this time, if the Court please,' Mason said, 'I move that this picture, which has previously been marked for identification as a defence exhibit, be introduced in evidence as a part of the defendant's case.'

'I object,' Hamilton Burger said. 'No proper foundation has been laid.'

Judge Madison smiled and said, 'Then I think I will sustain Mr Mason's objection to the question. I think this is a matter which calls for some investigation. It's highly technical but, nevertheless, it relates to the introduction of extraneous matter and the cross-examination of a witness on points which even the cross-examiner contends are irrelevant to the case.'

'It's not irrelevant on the *voir dire*,' Burger said.

'But the picture itself is irrelevant?'

'Yes.'

'Then,' Judge Madison said, 'if it wasn't ordered by the decedent, and it wasn't ordered by the defendant, what possible reason could there be for finding out who ordered it?'

'I want to know,' Hamilton Burger said. 'I'd like to satisfy my curiosity.'

'Your curiosity isn't one of the things that's in issue in this case,' Judge Madison said. 'I'm trying to restrict the evidence to pertinent questions. If you're going to object to the introduction of this picture, I presume you intend later on to move to strike out all evidence concerning the picture on the ground that it is incompetent, irrelevant, and immaterial.'

'That is true, Your Honour,' Burger said.

'Under those circumstances,' Judge Madison said, 'until this picture is further identified, I am not going to force this witness to divulge the names of his clients, particularly when it appears that the name of that client has nothing to do with the issues in this case. Or, to put it in another way, until there is something to make it appear that the name of the client would have anything to do with the issues. I think I will sustain the objection.

'However, it is so close to the hour of afternoon adjournment that I am going to hold the matter over until tomorrow morning. Quite frankly, I want to look up some of the authorities in regard to the right of cross-examination on extraneous evidence.'

Again Hamilton Burger had a brief, whispered conference with his associate, then said, 'If the Court please, I have no objection to the continuance. I, too, would like to look up some authorities. We will take the matter up in the morning.'

'Very well,' Judge Madison said. 'Court is adjourned until nine-thirty tomorrow morning.'

CHAPTER NINETEEN

Back in Mason's office the lawyer settled back into the cushioned swivel chair, stretched his arms above his head, heaved a deep sigh, and grinned.

'When you can take a gamble like that and come out, it's really something,' he said.

'What do you mean you've come out?' Drake said. 'You've just postponed the evil day of reckoning for a few hours. Tomorrow at nine-thirty you'll have to go back and face the same old situation.'

'Oh, no, I won't,' Mason said.

'What makes you think you won't?'

'In the first place,' Mason said, 'the word got around the courthouse that I was going to put the defendant on the stand in a preliminary hearing. That brought our old friend, Hamilton Burger, in for the kill.

'The fact that Hamilton Burger was coming in for the kill

caused all the newspaper reporters to attend the trial in order to see the showdown.'

'Well,' Drake said, 'since the showdown was postponed until tomorrow, the reporters will be there tomorrow and your client will be cross-examined and Hamilton Burger will want to know what it was Durant had on her that forced her to obey his wishes, and ask her if it is true that she would betray her friendships in order to save her own bacon; ask her if she didn't know she was participating in a swindling game, ask her if she didn't betray Rankin's friendship – he'll rip her to pieces.'

Mason said, 'I have news for you, Paul. There isn't going to be any tomorrow.'

'What do you mean?'

'Let's look at it logically. The whole thing snapped into shape as soon as I knew that Collin Durant didn't order that forged painting and that Goring Gilbert had never delivered it.'

'What does that have to do with it?'

'Everything.'

'All right,' Drake said. 'It was a skin game of some sort. Now, what was it?'

'It was an interesting skin game,' Mason said, 'but the person who ordered the forged painting and paid for it is the one who holds the key to the situation.'

'Who paid for the forged painting?' Drake asked.

Mason smiled and shook his head. 'We don't know – yet.'

'He's being mysterious, Paul,' Della Street said. 'He's going to play you like a trout. He'll have your curiosity aroused to fever pitch before he'll let you off the hook.'

'I'm at fever pitch now,' Drake said, 'and I don't get it.'

'All the factors are there,' Mason said. 'The painting was forged. It cost two thousand dollars. It was never delivered. The money was paid in hundred-dollar bills. Collin Durant had ten thousand dollars in hundred-dollar bills and got murdered.

'And I have a legal bombshell I can explode any minute now. I was tempted to do it today but I held my fire so I could make a big play on it.'

'What's the bombshell?' Drake asked. 'At least you can tell me that.'

'Finding the gun in the locker,' Mason said.

'Why, that clinches the case against Maxine,' Drake said. 'Those unidentified fingerprints aren't going to help. They could have been made at any time, either before or after.'

Mason smiled. 'Everyone has overlooked it,' he said.

'Overlooked what?'

'The lockers were serviced *every* twenty-four hours. Whenever they were inactive for any twenty-four-hour period they were opened. This locker had its twenty-four-hour inactive check on the evening of the fifteenth. Therefore, it was from the fourteenth to the fifteenth on which it was inactive. The gun had to be placed in it not on the thirteenth but on the fourteenth.

'That means the murderer planted the gun there *after* it became apparent Maxine had been seen there. The gun was planted *after* Maxine had left this part of the state, yet it was the murder weapon and, therefore, must have been left there by the real murderer.'

Drake's eyes widened.

'Well, I'll be a—'

The telephone rang sharply.

Della Street picked it up, said, 'Yes, Gertie. What is it? . . . Oh-oh . . . Just a minute.'

Della Street turned to Perry Mason. 'Mr Otto Olney is in the outer office and Gertie says he's mad. He's waving that subpoena around and wants to know what the devil you mean by serving a subpoena on him, that he has to be in Honolulu tomorrow.'

'Well,' Mason said, 'I guess we'll have to talk with him, but tell Gertie I'll see him within two to five minutes at the outside.'

Della Street relayed the message to Gertie.

'Can't you get in trouble serving a subpoena on a big businessman like that when you don't know exactly what you're going to ask him?'

'I know what I'm going to ask him,' Mason said. 'Get Lieutenant Tragg at Homicide for me, will you, Della?'

Della Street put through the call and a moment later said, 'Here's Lieutenant Tragg on the line.'

'Hello, Lieutenant,' Mason said. 'How's everything coming?'

'Coming very good indeed as far as we're concerned,' Tragg said cheerfully. 'I was sorry to see you put the defendant on the stand in a preliminary case like this, Mason.'

'Why?'

'Well, it's causing a lot of comment and I guess you probably realize that virtually none of it is favourable.'

'That's all right,' Mason said. 'I know you don't like to see me get in bad.'

'Actually I don't, Perry. You and I are pretty good friends, despite the fact we keep on the opposite side of the fence a good deal of the time.'

'Well,' Mason said, 'just in order to cement our friendship still further, I'd like to tell you who killed Collin Durant.'

'I think I already know,' Tragg said. 'I'm quite sure Hamilton Burger knows, and I think it's quite probable that Judge Madison knows.'

'Do you want to get a confession?'

'A confession would help things very much indeed,' Tragg said. 'What are you going to do, plead her guilty?'

'I don't know,' Mason said, 'but if you'll get up to my office right away, I'll give the matter some consideration. I have one client I've got to dispose of and then I'll be willing to give you all the help I can.'

'That's mighty nice of you,' Tragg said. 'I'll be up.'

'Now, don't misunderstand me,' Mason said. 'I said right away.'

'What do you mean by right away?'

'I mean *right* away.'

'Is it that important?'

'It's that important,' Mason said. '*Get up here!*'

The lawyer hung up the phone, grinned at the perturbed detective, said, 'Go to your office, Paul. I'll call you when I need you.'

He waited until Drake had left by the exit door, then said to Della, 'Ask Otto Olney to come in, if you will, please.'

Della Street went to the outer office and a moment later stepped to one side as the angry Olney strode past her.

'Look here, Mason, what the devil's the idea of serving a

subpoena on me in that murder case?' Olney asked.

'Frankly, I don't think Maxine did it. I'd like to see her beat the rap. When the case comes to trial in the Superior Court I'm going to check everything carefully and see if I know anything or if there's anything I can do, but I certainly am *not* going to perjure myself and I'm *not* going to go traipsing down to some little inferior court that doesn't have any discretion in the matter and make a spectacle out of myself trying to stick up for an artist's model.

'And remember, if you put any witnesses on the stand to testify on her behalf, the district attorney is just going to ask them if they ever saw her with her clothes off – and because she was an artist's model—'

'Did *you* ever see her with her clothes off?' Mason asked.

Olney said, 'As a matter of fact, I think I did, and damn it, Mason, that's not fair! My wife is very much— Well, this is a critical time for her and she's inclined to be ... well, insanely jealous.'

'Of course,' Mason said, 'I wouldn't want to cause any domestic discord.'

'I'm satisfied you wouldn't and I— Well, my lawyer, young Hollister at Warton, Warton, Cosgrove, and Hollister, was pretty much worked up about this. He wanted me to go to court and claim that you'd been abusing the process of the Court and a lot of things like that.

'Well, I just told him, nonsense. I said Mason's a reasonable man, he's got some grounds for what he wants to do, and I'm going up and see him and have a talk with him. I'll find out what it is he wants and I'll find out if there isn't some way we can help him.'

'Well,' Mason said, 'suppose *you* tell me just what *you* want.'

'I want to know what I can do to help you,' Olney said, 'and then I want you to give me a letter to the effect that you're releasing me from attendance on the court. For your information, I'm leaving for Honolulu on the ten o'clock plane tonight and then I may have to go on to the Orient.'

Mason looked at his watch, said, 'I'm expecting a visitor momentarily, Mr Olney. I'll hurry right along with this.

'Della, will you take this in shorthand, please?'

178

Della Street picked up her shorthand notebook and a pencil.

'A letter to Otto Olney, Esquire, with a copy to Judge Madison and a copy to Hollister of Warton, Warton, Cosgrove, and Hollister. "Dear Mr Olney: Upon receipt of your assurance this afternoon that you knew nothing about the case, nothing about the false Phellipe Feteet painting, that you didn't know Goring Gilbert, who was painting the copy, knew nothing about the copy being painted, and had no business contacts with Collin Durant, I have agreed to release you from attendance in court tomorrow in the case of People versus Maxine Lindsay, and agree to recall the subpoena which has been served on you and permit you to leave the jurisdiction of the court."'

Mason hesitated a minute, said, 'I think that covers it, doesn't it, Olney? I'd like to have you ask Hollister over to check it.'

'I think it covers the situation,' Olney said. 'There's no need for Hollister, and I want to apologize to you, Mr Mason, for flying off the handle a little. I guess I . . . well, I got a little worked up about it.'

'That's all right,' Mason said, 'and Della, you probably had better put a little note at the bottom of that to be signed by Mr Olney, stating quote, I assure you that the facts mentioned by you in the letter are correct and that I have given you my assurance I have no knowledge of any of the matters mentioned.'

Mason hesitated a moment, then said, 'I think that covers it. Make a blank for Mr Olney to sign, type the words "Otto Olney" underneath the blank, and I guess that's all. Can you get that letter out right away?'

'Within a very few minutes,' Della Street said, watching Mason's face curiously to see if he was giving her some signal.

Mason, completely poker-faced, nodded. 'Go right ahead, Della.'

Della looked from Mason to Olney. Mason took out his cigarette case, said, 'Want to smoke, Mr Olney?'

'No, thank you,' Olney said. 'I'll be on my way. I've got a lot of things to do— Oh, I suppose you want me to sign that letter and I suppose I should have that letter in my possession in case anything is said about my disregarding the subpoena.'

'Yes. You'll have to wait for it,' Mason said. 'But it will only be a few minutes. Don't you think you'd better check with Hollister?'

Olney looked at his watch, started to say something, changed his mind, settled back in the chair and said, 'No need to bother Hollister. I'll handle this. All of this has, of course, come as a terrific shock to me. I put great value on that Phellipe Feteet painting. I have instructed Rankin to buy more of them if he can find them at anything like a reasonable price. I'm telling you that in confidence, Mr Mason, it's not to be given to the Press.'

'I understand,' Mason said.

'I'm a nut on Phellipe Feteet,' Olney confessed. 'I wouldn't take a hundred thousand for that one painting I have, and I'll pay up to thirty thousand for any more.'

Mason said, 'This man Goring Gilbert is quite a character. The man has a remarkable amount of ability. He's made a copy of your Phellipe Feteet that is really remarkable.'

Olney said, 'I'd like to correct you on one thing, if I might, Mr Mason. It isn't a copy, it's a forgery.'

'Wouldn't it be difficult to make a forgery of that sort from memory?' Mason asked.

'I assume that it would. I suppose, however, that there are coloured photographs available of the painting. After all, it had had two prior owners before me.'

'I assume so,' Mason said, 'but it certainly takes a high degree of skill to copy a painting of that sort, no matter how it's done.'

'I most certainly agree with you on that,' Olney said.

Della Street returned with the letter.

Mason looked at it, passed it across to Olney and said, 'Sign right there, if you will, Mr Olney.'

Olney signed.

Mason said, 'I think, Della, that in order to satisfy the Court in this matter it would be a good plan to have Mr Olney swear – just hold up your right hand and swear that the facts contained in that letter are true, Mr Olney. Della Street is a notary public.'

Olney said, 'Now, wait a minute. You didn't say anything about swearing.'

'It's just a formality,' Mason said. 'I think you'd better just put a notarial certificate on there, Della, and Mr Olney, if you'll hold up your right hand—'

Olney said, 'I don't sign anything under oath without consulting my attorney.'

'What's the difference between making a statement to me,' Mason asked, 'and swearing to it?'

'You know what the difference is.'

'Well, that statement is correct, isn't it?' Mason asked.

Olney said, 'I've told you my position, Mr Mason. Right now I'm not certain that I understand yours and if I do understand it, I'm not certain I appreciate it.'

'Well, if you don't appreciate it, perhaps you don't understand it,' Mason said. 'By the way, I'm trying to find out where Durant got those one-hundred-dollar bills. You know, a man can't just pick up a lot of one-hundred-dollar bills by walking into some place of business and asking to cash a cheque, and those bills must have come from a bank.'

'I would assume so,' Olney said, his eyes studying Mason with sudden wariness.

'I'll tell you what,' Mason said. 'You can make an affidavit for me and I'll use that affidavit to present to the Court tomorrow, an affidavit that you know nothing whatever about the case, that you didn't give Durant any one-hundred-dollar bills, that you didn't—'

'Who says I didn't give him any hundred-dollar bills?' Olney asked suddenly.

'Why, you mentioned in the letter there that you didn't have any business transactions with him.'

'Well, that doesn't— Well, I didn't, but— Well, I *could* have loaned the man money.'

'Did you?' Mason asked.

'I think that's a matter I don't care to discuss at the moment, Mr Mason.'

Mason said, 'Gosh, Olney, I'm sorry. If you gave him any money in the form of hundred-dollar bills, you're going to have to go to court tomorrow.'

Olney said, 'Now, wait a minute, Mason. You told me I didn't have to go to court.'

'Predicated on your assurance that you knew nothing about the matter and had had no business transactions with Durant,' Mason said.

The door from the outer office opened, and Lt Tragg came bustling in. 'All right, Perry,' he said. 'You told me to get here and I got here. I had to violate a few police regulations in regard to code one and the use of siren and red spotlight in order to do it, but here I am.'

'Well, that's fine,' Mason said. 'You know Mr Olney, Lieutenant Tragg?'

'I know him,' Tragg said.

'Olney has just told me,' Mason said, 'that he loaned Durant some money in the form of hundred-dollar bills. How much was it, Mr Olney?'

Olney said, 'Now wait a minute. What is this? I'm not going to be interrogated here, and furthermore I didn't tell you any such thing.'

'I certainly understood you to say that you had given Durant some one-hundred-dollar bills,' Mason said.

'I said I *could* have. I *could* have advanced the man some money. I could have cashed a cheque.'

'Did you?' Mason asked, catching Lt Tragg's eye.

'Actually I ... I felt sorry for the guy and it's for that reason that I was so absolutely astounded when he made that statement disparaging the authenticity of my Phellipe Feteet painting. That's one of the most prized paintings in my entire collection.'

'Then may I ask just how much money you gave him from time to time and when you gave it to him?'

'You may not,' Olney said, 'and the more I see of your attitude, Mr Mason, the more I realize that I made a mistake in trusting you and coming here without my attorney. I'm going to call my lawyer and—'

'Now, just a minute,' Lt Tragg interrupted. 'If you're not going to tell Mr Mason about this, you'd better tell me. Durant had ten thousand dollars, or just about ten thousand dollars, on him when he was found dead. Now, how much of that came from you?'

Olney said, 'Who said any of it came from me?'

'Nobody said that,' Tragg said, 'I'm asking you how much

of it came from you. Now be careful what you say. This is a murder case, Olney.'

'You have no right to get me up here and start badgering me.'

'I'm not badgering you,' Tragg said, 'I'm investigating a murder case. I'm asking a question. I didn't get you up here. You came up here.'

'Well, your question is one I don't intend to answer. Not that I have anything to conceal, but I have some complicated business transactions and I just have a general understanding that I won't do anything without my attorney.'

'Then you'd better telephone your attorney and ask him to come over here,' Mason said. 'Miss Street can do it for you. Della, will you ring up Mr Hollister and tell him that Olney would like to have him over here?'

'Don't do it,' Olney said. 'I don't want him over here. I'm going over there. I'm going to talk with him before I say anything to anybody.'

'That Feteet was the prize of your collection?' Mason asked.

'It certainly was.'

'And how did it happen that you didn't miss it for the week it was gone from the yacht, during which Goring Gilbert was copying it down in his studio?'

'Who said it was missing from the yacht?'

'It had to be,' Mason said.

Tragg said, 'I'm interested in knowing how much of the money that Durant had on him came from you, and with all due deference to your position, Mr Olney, I intend to find out before you leave this office.'

'Well, I don't have to tell you anything before I leave this office.'

'No, you don't,' Tragg said, 'but if you don't, it's rather a suspicious circumstance.'

'What's suspicious about it?'

'Why should you give him ten thousand dollars?' Tragg asked. 'Was he blackmailing you?'

'What do you mean?' Olney asked.

Mason said, 'Tragg, you might ask him if it isn't true that

he commissioned Gilbert to make a copy of the Phellipe Feteet painting.'

'Why should I want anyone to make a copy of my painting?' Olney asked.

'Probably,' Mason said, 'because you were in domestic difficulties, knew that your wife was planning to file suit for divorce, and you intended to make certain she didn't get your most cherished painting.'

Olney said, 'Do you realize what you're saying? Do you realize that you have accused me of—'

'Exactly,' Mason said, 'and if you don't tell the complete story you're apt to find yourself accused of murder. Lieutenant Tragg wasn't born yesterday. And I served a subpoena on your wife a short time ago.'

Olney's face turned white. 'You subpoenaed my wife in this case?'

'Yes.'

'Oh, my God!' Olney exclaimed. 'Now the fat *will* be in the fire!'

Mason glanced at Tragg, said, 'On the day of his murder, Collin Durant didn't have any funds at all at about six o'clock in the evening. By the time of his death, probably around eight o'clock in the evening, he had ten thousand dollars in hundred-dollar bills. Banks weren't open at that time. Now, you just tell us whether you gave him those one-hundred-dollar bills.'

'Yes,' Lt Tragg said, 'I think that will be a very good starting point.'

Olney got to his feet, stood for a moment, then said, 'I am going to see my attorney.'

'I beg your pardon,' Tragg said, '*you're* not going anywhere. You're going to police headquarters with me if you aren't going to answer that question. I'm making it official now. I'm asking you if Durant got that money from you.'

'Yes,' Olney said at length. 'He got it from me.'

'Now, that's better,' Tragg said. 'When did he get it?'

'He got it about seven-forty-five.'

'And why did he get it?'

'He told me if he had the money he could . . . well, he could get Maxine Lindsay to disappear.'

184

'And why did you want her to disappear?'

'Because I couldn't afford to go ahead with the lawsuit I'd filed over that damned phoney painting and I couldn't afford to back up on it.'

'Now then,' Tragg said, 'you're beginning to make a little sense. So you saw Durant at seven-forty-five?'

'Yes.'

'Where?'

'In front of the apartment house where Maxine Lindsay lived.'

'Then,' Mason said, smiling at Lt Tragg, 'so far as is known, Olney, you were the last person to see Durant alive, because Maxine Lindsay has a perfect alibi from seven-forty-five. She was at the bus terminal at eight o'clock.'

'You don't know what she did *after* that,' Olney said defiantly. 'The medical testimony is that Durant could have been killed any time up to eight-twenty.'

'I think you'd better tell us about what *you* did,' Lt Tragg said. 'It might be a lot better that way, Mr Olney.'

'All right,' Olney said. 'I knew that I was coming to a showdown with my wife. She had all the evidence for a divorce. I didn't have any. I knew that she was going to strip me of my property – as much as she could.

'For some years I had been setting aside a cash reserve fund. I had nearly a quarter of a million dollars in safety deposit boxes that no one knew anything about. This money was in the form of hundred-dollar bills.

'Mason is correct. I wanted to keep my Phellipe Feteet.

'I guess I better put my cards right on the table with you gentlemen. It's my only chance now.

'I was in love. I've been in love for some time. My wife knew what was going on. She wouldn't give me a divorce. On the other hand, she used the power that the law gave her to hold a sword over my head. She wanted an absolutely impossible settlement. She wanted this settlement not to take care of herself, but to cause me the most suffering possible.

'She was threatening to file suit for separate maintenance, but not to file suit for divorce, not to give me my freedom. She was going to hold me in an impossible situation.

'I made up my mind that I'd try and buy her off, if I could.

185

I was willing to pay through the nose. Now, damn it, this is all highly confidential. Only my attorneys know anything about these negotiations.'

'Go ahead,' Tragg said. 'You're mixed up in a murder case now. You'd better come clean.'

'Well, I made up my mind that my wife was not going to get that particular painting, so I inquired around and found that there was a young man who was an expert at copying paintings. He could make forgeries that couldn't be told from the work of famous painters. He could copy every style of painting, and he could copy an original painting so that it was virtually impossible to tell the original and the copy apart.'

'That man was Goring Gilbert?' Tragg asked.

'I don't know who he was,' Olney said, 'but I assume it was. I hired a go-between because I couldn't afford to be identified with what was happening. This person made arrangements to have the painting copied. I paid two thousand dollars cash in hundred-dollar bills.'

'To Gilbert?' Mason asked.

'No, to the go-between.'

'That was Durant?' Tragg asked.

'It very definitely was *not* Durant. I wouldn't have touched Durant with a ten-foot pole. He was a slimy double-crosser. I wouldn't have put myself in his power for a minute.'

'Then how did it happen you gave Durant money?' Tragg asked.

'Because I walked into a trap. The first thing I knew, Durant had made this statement that my painting was a phoney. I got mad and made up my mind I'd teach him a lesson. Also, this was my chance to have my painting adjudged genuine. Then I could substitute the copy after I had established the authenticity of the original. So I just broke right into print and branded Durant a liar.

'Evidently that was exactly what he'd been waiting for. He showed up on the thirteenth and told me that he was going to subpoena Goring Gilbert, that he was going to claim I had commissioned Gilbert to make a copy of the painting, and that the copy was the one that was hanging in my yacht on the afternoon that he'd made the statement the painting was a forgery.

'Good heavens, I couldn't have that! My wife would have found out what was going on and the fat *would* have been in the fire. All right, I paid off. I paid through the nose. I gave that slimy, blackmailing upstart eleven thousand dollars.'

'Why eleven thousand dollars?' Mason asked.

'That was the price he demanded.'

'And when and where did you give it to him?'

'I met him in front of the apartment house which he designated and which I now know as the apartment house where Maxine lived. He said he had to give a part of the money to Maxine in order to keep the case from coming to a conclusion. He promised me that he'd see that she got out of town without making any statement. Then I could just fail to press the case and the matter would be closed.

'I distrusted Durant. I had a witness with me.'

'Let's find out exactly what happened,' Mason said. 'You met Durant in front of the apartment house?'

'Yes.'

'And you weren't alone?'

'No.'

'You paid him the money?'

'Not in front of the apartment house, no.'

'Where?'

'In Maxine's apartment.'

'You went up there?'

'Yes.'

'Who was with you?'

'This— A young lady was with me.'

'And you went up to Maxine's apartment?'

'Yes. He said he was going to give her money to get out of the state so she wouldn't be making any more statements and so you couldn't locate her. I didn't trust Durant for a minute. I went along to make sure he did what he said he was going to do.'

'You knocked on the door?'

'No, Durant had a key.'

'And what happened?'

'Maxine wasn't there. He said that he had hoped to catch her there before she went out.'

'What time was this?'

187

'Quarter to eight.'

'And what did you do?'

'I couldn't wait there for her to come back. I paid him the money – eleven thousand dollars. I had no other alternative.'

'That's an odd figure,' Mason said. 'Why eleven thousand?'

'He told me he'd borrowed a thousand dollars and that he'd have to give that money back in order to make things safe for all concerned; that he'd give Maxine money to travel with and then he'd let me dismiss the suit against him with prejudice and he'd see that Maxine said nothing to anyone.'

'So the three of you were in Maxine's apartment?'

'Yes.'

'And then what happened?'

'He remained there. We left. We went down to our car and drove several blocks and then this young woman who was with me remembered that she had left her purse. It was in the apartment. So she went back up to the apartment.'

'Go on,' Tragg said.

'When she got there she found the door partially open. She went in. Durant was dead. He was lying just as you found him. She was in a panic and opened the door to run and then saw that this nosy neighbour was standing in the hall. As it turns out, this woman was waiting for her boyfriend to come up in the elevator, but the young woman in question thought that she had heard something which had aroused her suspicions and was watching the Lindsay apartment and was about to call the police.'

'So what did she do?' Tragg asked.

'She did the only obvious thing she could think of. She's about the same size and build as Maxine. She dashed to the closet, found a voluminous, distinctive tweed coat, put it on, grabbed the canary and a package of birdseed, which was all tied up by the cage as though Maxine had been expecting someone to come and get the canary, and got out of the apartment, backing out so that she kept her back turned towards the woman in the hall, and hurried down to the stairs.'

'Then she joined me.'

Mason took a piece of paper, wrote on it.

Tragg said, 'All right, who's the young woman?'

Olney shook his head. 'Tragg,' he said, 'I'll go to prison, or anything else, but I'm not going to bring her into it.'

'Now, wait a minute,' Tragg said. 'Don't you realize this woman is the person who killed Durant? That is, if your story is true.'

'Nonsense!' Olney snapped. 'She wouldn't kill anyone – and she wouldn't lie to me.'

'Don't make a fool of yourself,' Tragg said. 'This is murder. You can't be like that.'

'I am like that, and I'm going to be like that,' Olney said.

Mason pushed the pad of paper, on which he had been writing, in front of Olney.

Olney took a look at the paper, then glared at Mason, but before he could say anything Mason said, 'Let's use our heads on this, Tragg. Durant had been doing business with Goring Gilbert. Durant had a bill at a paint store. He paid that off using hundred-dollar bills.

'That was shortly after the time Gilbert had received a fee in hundred-dollar bills from Olney's representative for making that false Feteet.

'Durant told Olney he had borrowed a thousand dollars and he'd have to repay that money. He must have borrowed that thousand from Gilbert.

'Now then, Olney paid Durant *eleven* thousand dollars. When they found Durant's body, he had *ten* thousand dollars on him. What happened to the extra thousand?'

'All right,' Tragg said, 'you're masterminding this. What do *you* think happened to it?'

'The murderer took it,' Mason said. 'The murderer was someone to whom Durant had a moral obligation to pay one thousand dollars. The murderer took the money. He didn't touch any more. The murderer was Goring Gilbert.'

'How did the murderer get in?' Tragg asked.

'Durant let him in,' Mason said. 'Gilbert was looking for Durant. He had reason to believe he'd find him at Maxine's apartment.

'Durant had put the first bite on Olney. From then on he intended to blackmail him as long as Olney's domestic affairs were in such a shape that he could.

'Gilbert didn't like the idea of Durant using the knowledge

189

he had about the false Feteet to blackmail Olney. He just wasn't going to stand for it.'

'How did Gilbert know about the blackmail?' Tragg asked.

'The same way he knew he'd find Durant in Maxine's apartment. Olney's friend arranged with Gilbert to copy the painting. When Durant put the bite on Olney, she phoned Gilbert and accused him of being in on the deal and told him Olney was to pay Durant eleven thousand dollars in front of Maxine's apartment house at seven-forty-five.

'Gilbert assured her this was all news to him. He knew Durant had seen the Feteet copy, but had no idea Durant was going to blackmail Olney. So Gilbert drove to a place in front of the apartment house where he could see for himself.

'When Olney and his friend left, Gilbert went up to have an accounting with Durant. Durant was such a cheap chiseller he had even swindled Maxine out of her get-away money, telling her to be out of the place by seven, then telling Olney to be there at seven-forty-five.'

Tragg snapped his fingers.

'Get it?' Mason asked.

'I've got it,' Tragg said, getting to his feet.

He turned to Olney. 'You're coming with me, Olney,' he said. 'I think this may get all straightened out, but until we get a confession you're a prime witness.'

Olney hesitated a moment, then said, 'Very well, I'll go with you. I'm satisfied it was Goring Gilbert. Durant had known he was copying the painting and had put two and two together, and that's why he rigged up this whole skin game so that I'd file suit against him.'

'You want to come, Mason?' Tragg asked. 'We could use a witness.'

'You're doing fine,' Mason said. 'Go right ahead.'

Mason got up and escorted Tragg to the door.

As he did so, Della Street picked up the paper on which Mason had written the name he had shown Olney – Corliss Kenner.

Della Street took Mason's desk lighter, snapped it into flame, and burnt the paper.

Mason returned from the door. 'Well,' he said, 'that's that.'

'You think he'll get a confession out of Gilbert?' Della Street asked.

Mason said, 'Della, don't ever discount the police. Once they get on the right trail they'll dig up what evidence they need. Remember the unidentified fingerprint on that locker. That, very definitely, would have been the fingerprint of Goring Gilbert. . . .'

'I can see now it had to be Gilbert,' she said. 'When he was paid for the picture, Durant was broke. Gilbert loaned him a thousand. Durant worked out the blackmailing game. Gilbert didn't like that. . . . How did he get Maxine's gun, Chief?'

'He found it,' Mason said. 'When he got into the apartment he went to the dresser to see if Maxine was in on the play and had left any incriminating evidence in the drawer. It was at that exact moment Durant started wondering if Olney had planned a trap and looked in the shower to see if a witness had been planted there.

'Gilbert found the gun – the temptation was too great. He despised Durant. . . . If he'd taken the whole eleven thousand it wouldn't have been such a giveaway. As it was, he took only the one thousand, thereby leaving a broad trail – to wit, the murdered didn't care much about money but was someone to whom Durant was indebted to the tune of an even thousand dollars.'

Della Street thought that over. 'And the hold Durant had on Maxine?'

'Durant,' Mason said, 'was the father of the child Maxine's sister had given birth to while the husband was overseas. Durant didn't care who knew it. Maxine did.'

Della Street nodded. 'I see now – and your fee?'

Mason grinned. 'You can send Howell's cheque back to him, Della. I think Olney will quite probably loan Maxine all she needs to cover costs.' Then after a moment he added, '*All* costs.'

GAVIN LYALL

'A complete master of
the suspense technique'
Liverpool Daily Post

SHOOTING SCRIPT
5/-
'The sky's the limit for this
fine suspense/adventure story'
Daily Mirror

MIDNIGHT PLUS ONE
5/-
'Grimly exciting . . . original
in concept, expertly written
and absolutely hair-raising'
New York Times

THE WRONG SIDE OF THE SKY
5/-
'One of the year's best
thrillers'
Daily Herald

'Thrillers on this level
are rare enough'
The Daily Telegraph